On The Rails

By Linda Shenton Matchett

To my parents

Richard M. and Jean W. Shenton

Thanks for believing in me.

Chapter One:

Schoolteacher Katherine Newman patted her wilting, Gibson-Girl pompadour and tugged at the high neck of her white cotton blouse. Her floor-length, navy-blue skirt blocked any chance of a breeze cooling her legs. Some of her modern friends had begun to eschew corsets, but Katherine's mother would have none of that.

Sighing, she glanced at the blackboard, chalk gripped in her right hand. Math equations filled the slate surface, yet her vision strayed to the sunshine beaming through the window. She met the eyes of an elderly gentleman grinning at her from the road. She smiled, and he tipped his hat before moving away.

Glancing past the fifteen upturned faces of the children to the clock on the wall in the back of the classroom, she pressed her lips together. One blessed hour until the bell would ring signaling the end of another school day. Another day closer to the end of the 1910 school year.

The students had been especially trying today. Several of the children hadn't done their homework, and Mary Robbins and Betsy Claiborne spent most of the day whispering. Katherine knew that Tommy Franklin was more inattentive than she was.

Shifting her attention back to the board, Katherine explained the math problems then distributed a practice exam that was met with groans from the children. "The sooner you finish, the sooner you can go outside and play."

The grumbling ceased, and the sound of scratching pencils filled the room.

Her gaze moved back to the street where she could see Willingham's Restaurant. Her heart quickened. In four hours, Henry Jorgenson, her boyfriend of ten months would take her there for dinner. She hadn't seen him since last Saturday when they enjoyed a picnic in Dorwin's Park.

How did she get so lucky that he wanted to court her? The nicest young man in town, he didn't drink, swear or play cards like the other boys. He treated her like a princess, bringing her small gifts or sending notes just to say he was thinking about her.

Surely, he was going to propose tonight. Why else would he take her to the best eating establishment in town?

She pressed a hand against her middle and took a deep breath. He would arrive at her house with his boots blacked, his face scrubbed to a shine, and his dark hair slicked down with pomade. He would help her into the carriage and murmur, "How beautiful you look in the moonlight." They would wave to their friends as the horse cantered down the street.

The carriage would stop, and Henry would help her from the conveyance, his touch gentle and warm. He'd lead her up the steps into the dimly lit rooms of the dining room. Crystal glassware would reflect the light from the massive chandelier in the center of the room. Creamy linen napkins would stand crisply folded at attention on each plate.

The maitre'd would nestle the couple at a small, corner table where they could share the details of their days with each other in private. After they sated their appetites, Henry would take her hand in his, stare into her eyes, and ask the magical question every woman wants to hear…

"Miss Newman, are you alright? May we be excused?" Jane Walton tugged at Katherine's skirt. "We're all finished. May be go outside now?"

"Hmmm?"

"Are you alright? Everyone turned in their tests, and it's almost time for the dismissal bell. We'd like to be excused."

"The bell? Yes, you may go. Be sure to take your homework assignments with you and be prepared to discuss them in class tomorrow." Katherine stuffed her books and the children's test papers into her worn satchel. She removed her tan cloak from its customary hook and wrapped it around her shoulders.

Even though spring was beginning to poke its sleepy head above the ground, the air still grew chilly during the late afternoons in the high country of Ohio. She pinned on her wide-brimmed, straw boater as she exited the schoolhouse.

Spotting her friend Claire who taught the first and second grade children, she waved and hastened to catch up with her.

Claire smiled. "You look a bit frazzled, Katherine. Let's stop and get a soda."

"I can't. I've got to get the students' tests graded before my date with Henry."

"On a school night?" Claire waggled her eyebrows at Katherine. "Are you allowed to do that?"

Katherine laughed. "I promise not to stay out too late."

"Where is he taking you?"

"The new place, Willingham's." She ducked her head. "I think he might propose tonight. We've been seeing each other for nearly a year, and the restaurant is very exclusive. Why else would he take me there?"

"How exciting! Then you can stop teaching. Sometimes I wish I could."

"The kids make us crazy, don't they? I wish the laws were different, and women didn't have to quit work after they married. I love my students. Seeing their faces light up when they learn new concepts is such a joy. That's why I entered teaching in the first place. I worked hard to earn my certificate. It seems irresponsible to put it in a drawer just because I'm married."

"Katherine! You'd be taking a job away from an unmarried woman who needs to support herself. You can't be selfish."

"I know." Katherine sighed." It's just a shame."

Claire winked. "Taking care of Henry will require all your energy. You won't have time for anything else."

"That's for sure. And I'll have to make our new house a home…sewing curtains and quilts, putting in the vegetable garden, and helping him with the animals." Her face warmed. "I'd like lots of children, too."

"That's what every woman wants, isn't it?" Claire nudged Katherine's shoulder.

"After Henry asks, you should let him stew for a day or two. Tell him you need time to decide."

"I couldn't do that. That would be dishonest. And I love him too much to do something like that."

Claire sobered. "Katherine, are you sure Henry is going to ask you to marry him? You've only been seeing each other since July. Wouldn't a proposal be rushing things?"

"Of course, he's going to propose. Why else would he choose the most exclusive restaurant in town?" Katherine moistened her dry lips. Was Claire right? Was it too soon to expect a proposal?

Henry stopped the wagon in front of the restaurant. He set the brake then jumped down and helped Katherine climb from the vehicle. They ascended the stairs and entered the brightly-lit building.

"Katherine! Henry!" Matilda Watson surged toward them, her stately figure cutting between the tables like a scythe. "Imagine seeing you here."

Henry stiffened. Matilda will ensure everyone knows what transpired tonight. He pasted a smile on his face and bowed. "It's good to see you, too. Is Mr. Watson here?"

"Of course, he is, silly boy. We're seated by the window. The best table in the house." Her chin quivered as her head bobbed back and forth between Katherine and Henry. Large, dangling gold earrings bounced with every motion, and her bejeweled fingers clasped and unclasped in staccato motion. Matilda had underestimated her dress size, and the sapphire outfit pulled and bulged in several unfortunate places.

The maître d' gestured to Henry. "Pardon the interruption, Mr. Jorgenson, but your table is ready."

Henry unclenched his jaw. "A pleasure to see you, Mrs. Watson. Enjoy your dinner."

"I'm sure we will, young man. And you two enjoy your romantic interlude!"

Henry bit his lip and followed the maître d'. The old busybody couldn't possibly speak any louder.

After they were seated, Katherine leaned across the table. "Don't worry about disturbing the other diners. They're familiar with our Mrs. Watson."

"You're right. I worry too much about what others think. Let's forget about Mrs. Watson and make our selections." Would Katherine be as gracious during their after-dinner conversation?

Henry placed his silverware on the empty plate. He wiped his mouth and laid the linen napkin on the table. Their meal has passed too quickly. It was time.

After clearing his throat, he took a deep breath.

Katherine smiled at him, a look of expectancy on her face.

He swallowed past the growing lump in his throat. "Katherine, you are a wonderful woman. I have always been surprised and humbled by the fact you are willing to go out with me. You have made me a better man." Henry fiddled with the edge of his dinner napkin. "But you deserve someone better, someone who is your intellectual equal and can provide you with a home and financial security. What I'm trying to say is that we can no longer see each other."

Katherine gaped at Henry. Tears sprang to her eyes, and heat suffused her face.

He was breaking up with her. She was a fool to think tonight's date would end in a marriage proposal, to think he wanted to make her his wife.

"Katherine, I'm sorry. I know I've hurt you--"

She clamored from the chair and rose to her full five-foot-two-inch height. She looked down her nose at him, and he jumped to his feet.

How dare he break up with her in such a public place? Was that to prevent her from making a scene? Katherine's gaze swept the room. The ever-vigilant Mrs. Watson stared at the two of them.

Katherine's breath caught. She must escape, but first...

Opening her hand, she swung her arm forward and slapped Henry's right cheek.

The resounding crack filled the room and silenced the buzz of conversation. Needles of pain stung her palm and shot up her arm, but the red imprint of her hand on his face soothed the burn as no balm could.

"I'll see myself home, Mr. Jorgenson." Now, if she could manage to leave the room without dissolving in a puddle of tears.

Chapter Two

Katherine gripped her basket and crossed the dusty street from the schoolhouse to the general store. She wiped a stray tear from her cheek and stiffened her spine. It had been two weeks since her dinner with Henry. No one needed to know her heart still ached from their breakup. Would the pain ever go away? Would she find another man she would love as much as she loved Henry?

Mom assured her with the age-old cliché that there were other fish in the sea. Katherine nibbled her lower lip. She didn't want another fish. She wanted Henry.

Katherine hurried up the steps of the shop, and her toe caught the top tread. Falling in a heap on the porch, she landed on her hip. Her skirt fanned out around her, and her hat fell forward over her face.

Giggling sounded behind her. Katherine gritted her teeth as she struggled to her feet, her hip and ankle throbbing. She looked over her shoulder. Two of her students watched her from the street with broad smiles on their faces.

Shoving her boater on top of her head, Katherine searched for her basket. The handle peeked out from under one of the wooden rocking chairs that lined the verandah. She snatched it from its hiding place and limped through the door, the children's voices fading. Could this day get any worse?

"Good afternoon, Miss Newman. You all right?" The shopkeeper, Silas Greene, grinned at her from behind the counter. With his front row seat to the window, he had obviously seen her tumble. What sort of man laughs at a woman in trouble?

"I'm just fine, Mr. Greene." She lifted her chin and glared at him. "Here to pick up some items for the family."

"I expect you'd like me to put everything on your father's account."

With a curt nod, she gestured to the back room. "Has the new dress material arrived yet?"

"Yes, miss. Several bolts of fabric came in yesterday's delivery. Some mighty fine choices."

Turning, Katherine sauntered along the shelves. Consulting her mother's list, she selected a variety of items and tucked them into her basket. After she had exhausted the list, she strolled into the room that held sewing supplies.

"Did you hear about that poor Katherine Newman? Henry Jorgensen is no longer courting her."

"I did hear the news." The woman tittered. "And no one seems to know why he changed his mind. What do you think happened? She seems like such a nice girl."

The voices came from behind the rack of fabric. A chill swept over Katherine, and she froze in her tracks. Should she make her presence known or find out what sort of gossip was circulating about her?

"Her family acts like they are better than everyone else. Perhaps Henry got tired of having to prove himself."

Katherine pressed her hand over her mouth. Is that what the townspeople thought about her family? She huddled behind a shelf.

"You think so?"

"Who knows? She also has a bit of a temper. No one wants to live with a shrew."

"A temper? You don't say."

"Yes, she slapped Henry in public. Can you imagine? No woman of integrity does that."

"Tsk. It is a shame she isn't better behaved. It's a good thing Henry realized his mistake before saying 'I do.' He's a smart young man."

Biting back a sob, Katherine hurried from the room. She didn't have a temper, did she? Henry deserved the slap. He had embarrassed her in public, and now women in town were dissecting her behavior. How many other people were talking about her?

"I've got to get away. Leave town and start over. Somewhere no one knows me." She expelled a deep breath. "What am I thinking? I've never traveled by myself. What sort of woman does that?"

Her shoulders slumped. "I'm trapped."

Henry ladled steaming soup into a bowl and passed it down the table. The large crock was filled to the rim with potatoes, cabbage and beans. Bits of ham floated in the mixture. Thick slices of fresh-baked dark, crusty bread topped off the meal.

His family crowded around the table and jostled each other as they vied for attention. Giggles and shouts undulated around him. The voices slowly built to a crescendo as the competition to be heard rose. Heat from the cook stove and the crowd of bodies in the room gave the room a tropical feel. Henry hunched over his food. When would his heart stop hurting? Surely, breaking up with Katherine had been the right thing to do. Hadn't it? She deserved a better man.

A knock sounded, and Henry's sister, Alice, rose and opened the door to find Bruce Brown, their landlord's property manager standing on the porch wearing a rumpled, tan tweed suit and clutching a large envelope. A slightly stooped man with a small mustache and a laurel wreath of sandy-colored hair framing his oval-shaped head, Brown had hooded, beady eyes that constantly moved back and forth.

"Won't you come in, Mr. Brown?" Alice stepped back.

"Thank you, Miss Jorgenson. I'm here to speak with your parents." The property manager seemed to make an attempt to smooth out the wrinkles in his jacket.

"You're certainly formal tonight, Bruce." Henry, Sr. stood, a frown etched on his face. "Is everything all right? Won't you join us for dinner?"

"No thank you. I only need a moment. Is there somewhere we can talk in private?"

"We have no secrets in this house, Bruce. Please sit down. Dinner isn't much, but we would like to eat it while it is still warm," said Olga.

Henry pulled another chair up to the table and eyed Bruce as he plopped into the seat.

The manager pulled at the collar of his shirt. "There's no easy way to tell you, so I'll just say it. Mr. Swenson is calling in his loan. You need to pay him the remainder of the mortgage by the end of the summer."

"What?" Henry, Sr. sputtered. "Why is he calling in our loan? We've lived here for years and faithfully made our payment every month, even when times have been tough and the farm was barely supporting its way."

"You've only been making the interest payments for the last year, and that's not acceptable. These papers have all the details."

"How could he do this?"

"I'm not privy to Mr. Swenson's affairs, Henry. I simply collect the payments. He can do whatever he wishes with his financials."

"But it's not fair, Bruce. Is it possible to meet with him to discuss this?"

"No, his mind is made up. You have until August thirty-first to satisfy the loan. If you have any questions, you know where you can reach me. Good night, Henry, Olga."

He stood, bowed, and hurried out of the house.

Henry stared at his father. "What are we going to do?"

Katherine pushed her food around on her plate as her father reached for the pot roast platter. She swallowed against the lump in her throat. Hopefully no one would notice she wasn't eating.

"Katherine, aren't you hungry this evening?" Her mother's brow furrowed.

So much for no one noticing. "It must be the heat."

"More for me." Her father's eyes crinkled at the corners as he smiled. "You girls don't want any more of this, right?"

"George, that's your third helping."

"Help yourself, Daddy." Elizabeth pointed to the food on her plate. "We've had more than enough."

"Keep up your strength, Dad." Katherine forced a smile on her lips. "That after-dinner newspaper is heavy, isn't it?"

"I need all my stamina to raise you girls." He winked at her.

"Katherine, you need to eat. You've lost weight since Henry broke up with you."

Dropping her fork, Katherine pushed her chair away from the table. "I don't know what to do. I feel like I'm drowning in pity. Everyone knows about my breakup with Henry and seems to avoid me. Women stop talking when they see me. I overheard two women in the mercantile today say terrible things about me. School seems like a chore. It's all I can do each morning to get up and go teach." Her eyes filled with tears. "I'm cornered with no way out."

Katherine's mother reached over and squeezed her hand. "Honey, your father and I have been thinking about this situation. You haven't been yourself since it happened."

"I thought I managed to put up a good front."

Elizabeth cocked her head. "You're no fun anymore. You never laugh, and you hardly ever speak. You spend a lot of time staring at nothing. I didn't want to say anything because I didn't want to hurt your feelings. You did right by slapping Henry."

"Elizabeth!" Their mother frowned.

"What? You know I'm right."

"I've considered going to his home and giving him a piece of my mind, but that would only give the ladies something else to talk about."

Katherine dried her eyes with a napkin. "You're the best family a girl could wish for. I was starting to wonder if I was losing my mind."

"It's easy to get over a scraped knee or sprained ankle, honey. A broken heart takes much longer to heal. Dad and I think you need a change of scenery and to do something with girls your own age." Her mother's eyes sparkled. "We have the perfect solution."

"You do?" Katherine sniffled. "I only know how to teach. How is that going to get me with people my own age?"

Mom reached out and took her hand. "Do you remember what I used to do before I married your father?"

"You were a waitress." She tilted her head. "You want me to wait tables?"

"I was more than a waitress." Mom squared her shoulders. "I was a Harvey Girl."

"There's a difference?"

"Yes, indeed. Fred Harvey established his own idea of the working woman, and I'm proud to have been part of that. His employees were never called waitresses. We were Harvey Girls and expected to act as such twenty-four hours a day. We were told where to live, what time to go to bed, who we could date, even what to wear down to the last detail of makeup and jewelry." Her face glowed. "It was our job to ensure the railroad passengers had the perfect dining experience when they stepped into our dining rooms. Fred Harvey treated his employees better than anyone I know. Promotions were given fair and square, and even guaranteed if an employee remained on the payroll for a certain number of years. We worked our way up through a house and wore badges with numbers indicating our position among the servers."

"I didn't realize that, Mom."

"There's even more. A Harvey Girl could eventually become a head waitress, which meant better pay, a different uniform, and her own room in the dormitory. If a woman stayed in the system long enough, she could even become a manger. Female managers were rare, but they were treated equally in terms of job description and pay. We could even transfer to other locations if we wanted to."

"How come you never told us any of this, Mom?"

"It was a long time ago, Katherine. I didn't think you girls would be interested." She waved her hand. "Anyway, your father was reading the paper a couple of weeks ago and ran across an ad in the Help Wanted section. There are new Harvey Houses in Arizona, and they're looking for additional staff. I wrote to my old manager who works in the Chicago office now, and he agreed to hire you if you want the job. You fit the bill perfectly. Mr. Harvey's applicants must have completed at least eighth grade, exhibit good manners, clear speech, and neatness. You could start as soon as school dismisses for the summer."

Katherine sagged against the chair. Tears started afresh. "You did this for me?"

Her mom rose and wrapped her arms around Katherine. "I would do anything for you, and you've been so unhappy."

Her palms slicked. "You think I can do this?"

"Absolutely. You're a smart girl."

Katherine dried her eyes. "Then it's settled. Notify your manager he can expect me by June thirtieth." What was she getting herself into?

Olga Jorgenson cleared the dishes off the table. After Bruce's announcement, her family spent the remainder of the meal picking at their food. She didn't bother to offer this afternoon's bread pudding. The girls scraped the leavings into the pig's bucket.

Henry, Sr. leaned on the wooden mantle above the large stone fireplace. "Sit down. We need to discuss our situation before it gets much later." He knocked the burnt tobacco out of his pipe before refilling it. He held a match to the bowl and took a long drag on the stem before reading the documents Bruce had left behind. "Even with our troubles, morning comes early on the farm, and we must be up with first light."

The younger three children crowded around Olga who sat in the rocker their father had made when Henry, Jr. was born. Alice and Gladys huddled together on the worn couch next to Carl who stared at the floor. Henry, Jr. sat on the floor near the couch.

Henry, Sr. took another draw on the pipe. "The situation seems dire, but your mother and I have had tough times before. We'll weather this storm. If we work together, we can raise enough money to pay Mr. Swenson." His eyes swept over the occupants in the room.

"We could lease the lower field to Joe Branding."

"We could sell the farm and move to a smaller place."

"How about if we sell the farm and move out west?"

"We could all get jobs."

"What about a yard sale, Dad?" John sold some of his toys at the town's rummage sale last year and thought $5.00 was a lot of money.

Henry, Sr. smiled at his youngest. "That's a great idea, son, every little bit will help."

"Don't be ridiculous, Dad, we won't get enough money from a yard sale," Carl snapped.

"We all need to have a hand in solving this problem, and a yard sale is the extent of John's ability to contribute. What are you going to do?"

"Henry and I talked about applying for work at the mines. They pay top dollar for the night crew, and we can still help out here on the farm."

"That's mighty generous, son, but you've got to sleep sometime."

"We'll take turns working during the day, Dad." Henry said.

"Alice and I will take in washing. We'll make the rounds of the townspeople tomorrow. That way we can be here to help Mother."

"Frank and I will help John with the rummage sale." Audrey piped up.

"These are all wonderful ways you can help. Your mother and I appreciate your willingness to help out. We don't want to sell the farm. We've lived here a long time. It would be hard to start over, don't you think? We've got nearly three months till the end of August. Let's meet again on July fifteenth. We can see how much money we've saved and decide what to do at that time. How does that sound?"

"It's a good thing I've already stopped courting Katherine, don't you think?"

Henry, Jr. slumped against the sofa.

Olga reached toward her son. "Oh, Henry—"

Henry leapt to his feet. "I don't need your pity." He yanked open the front door and rushed out into the night.

Chapter Three

Katherine found her seat on the train then poked her head out the window to wave at her family. Mom dabbed at her eyes with a handkerchief, and Dad's face was flushed. Elizabeth grinned and pointed to the handsome man climbing the steps into the car. Katherine shook her head and blinked away her tears. Pressing a hand against her middle, she took a deep breath.

She was a grown woman, and people traveled cross-country by rail all the time. There was nothing to be frightened of. Too bad the swarm of hummingbirds in her stomach didn't seem to know that. The train swayed and rattled as the wheels churned. Steam billowed, and her parents were enveloped in the white fog on the platform. The iron behemoth chugged forward and was soon hurtling toward open country.

Clickety-clack. Clickety-clack.

Katherine glanced at the other passengers and rubbed her arms. What did the

future hold? Across the aisle sat a young woman who looked to be her own age. She smiled, and Katherine nodded.

Trains had not changed much in the two years since her father had escorted her back from Teacher's College. Twenty rows of seats were covered in heavy, navy-blue fabric. Light fixtures in frosted globes lined the ceiling every three to four feet. A wire luggage rack above the seats ran the entire length of the coach. Green canvas shades hung at each window. A floral picture in an ornate gilded frame hung at the back near the doorway to the next car. She would investigate her sleeper later.

"Is this your first time traveling?"

Katherine turned toward the voice.

The young woman across the aisle leaned toward her. "I'm Eunice."

"I'm Katherine. I came home from normal school on a train, but it was only a three-hour journey. Have you ridden a train before?"

"When I was a small child, we went to my grandfather's funeral. It took two days to get there. I don't remember much." Eunice extended her hand. "I'm going to Arizona. Where are you going?"

"I'm also going to Arizona." Katherine tilted her head. "Are you a Harvey girl?"

"Yes." Eunice blushed. "Well, I will be when I arrive."

Katherine scooted to the aisle seat. "Me, too. My mother was a Harvey Girl. That's how I got the job."

"I answered an advertisement in the newspaper. I don't know much about them."

"According to my mother, Fred Harvey – that's the man behind the Harvey Houses – emigrated from England sometime around 1850. He worked a bunch of jobs, mostly in the restaurant business. After the Civil War, he traveled across the country using the railroad system. He thought the food service was terrible, so he set up a couple of small cafes on the Kansas Pacific Railroad. Then he made an arrangement with the Santa Fe Railroad, and the company has been putting up Harvey Houses along their routes ever since."

"How smart of him."

"He passed away about ten years ago, but his son operates the company now. There are Harvey Houses about every hundred miles."

Eunice clapped her hands. "We're going to be part of something big, aren't we?"

Two days later, the train pulled to a stop. The porter strolled through the car. "Williams, Arizona. This is the Williams, Arizona station. Everyone out for Williams." He opened the door and stepped onto the platform.

Katherine and Eunice gathered their belongings and hastened out the door of the coach. Katherine gawked at the crowd. Men in uniform threaded their way among cowboys. Women and children laughed and talked. Indians. Lots of Indians.

Eunice elbowed her. "Stop staring."

Katherine's face warmed. "Sorry."

A woman approached, her brow furrowed. "Are you girls here to work at the Harvey House?" Her blonde hair was drawn into a severe knot at the back of her head. She wore a black dress and carried a large folder of papers.

"Yes, ma'm." Katherine stifled the urge to curtsy.

"Good. I am the House Manager, Evelyn Stewart. You may call me Miss Stewart. Please indicate which bags are yours, and I'll have our man bring them to your rooms."

Eunice and Katherine pointed at their trunks stacked on the platform with dozens of other suitcases.

"Welcome to the Harvey family. I hope you ladies are used to hard work."

Chapter Four

Rushing to catch up with Miss Stewart, Katherine glanced at the collection of attached buildings that spread for two blocks along the railroad tracks. Each structure was square-shaped and rose three stories toward the sky. Passing under a seventy-five-foot portico with plain white columns, she hurried through the mahogany door that featured leaded-glass windows etched with the Harvey logo. Everywhere she looked brass hardware gleamed.

Her feet sinking into the plush burgundy carpet, Katherine grinned at Eunice. This Harvey House was a palace. Large oil paintings hung on the walls in gilt frames, and carved oak furniture with brocade cushions filled the rooms. Exotic plants and greenery accented the beautiful furnishings. Burgundy drapes held in place with silk cords graced the floor-to-ceiling windows.

The trio trooped upstairs, and Miss Stewart stopped in front of an open door. She gestured inside. "This is your room. Take a few moments to freshen up, but you must be back in the foyer—" She glanced at the small, gold watch pinned on her bodice. "In thirty minutes."

"Yes, ma'am."

"Very good." Miss Stewart pivoted and left the room on silent feet.

"For someone in the hospitality business, she's not too hospitable," Eunice whispered.

Katherine giggled. "Shhh. She might hear you." She dropped onto one of the twin beds and stretched. "I'm finally here."

Eunice poured water from the pitcher in the bowl on the dresser then dunked one of the small cloths into the liquid and rinsed her face. "Ahh. It must be ninety degrees outside."

"Probably more. My mom said the temperatures can soar above one hundred during the summer."

Dabbing at her face with a dry towel, Eunice's voice was muffled. "Miss Stewart seems rather strict."

"She does, but after we've made the grade, she'll lighten up."

Eunice looked at Katherine. "Do you think so?"

Katherine shrugged. What had she gotten herself into?

Katherine and Eunice entered the immense dining room filled with dozens of tables surrounded by large walnut chairs with cane seats and covered in crisp, white cloths. The tableware sparkled in the sunlight streaming from the windows. The room was vacant save a lone man watering a jungle of plants that lined the walls. Expectancy and readiness hung in the air.

Miss Stewart peered at Eunice and Katherine. "Thank you for your promptness. You will begin work tomorrow. Uniforms will be delivered to your room. Pay strict attention to what I am about to say. I will not repeat myself."

Her arm made a sweeping motion over the room. "Harvey Houses are outfitted with only the finest furnishings and linens. The furniture is hand-carved and imported from England. Our linens are handmade and come from Belfast, Ireland. The napkins are made with an exclusive pattern to match our china which is also imported, and they are oversized to accommodate gentlemen who wish to tuck them into their waistcoats."

She led them around the room. "Your contracts come with obligations that must be adhered to. You will live in Dormitory B with House Mother Mrs. Lindsay. Curfew is at ten o'clock and is enforced with no exceptions. After you have been here for three months, you may seek special permission to stay out later, but the doors will be locked at curfew. Your room is to be kept immaculate, and you are responsible for your own laundry with the exception of your uniform. The company will clean them three times a week, however, it is your job to starch and iron them."

Miss Stewart peered at the girls, and Katherine nodded. Her head swam. "Should I be taking notes, Miss Stewart?"

"Certainly, you can remember a few rules, Miss Newman."

"Yes, ma'am." Did the woman have no heart?

"Very good. Now, the head waitress, Nora Washington, will train you in your specific duties, however, I will cover some of the generalities. You are to wear your numbered badge at all time. You will work twelve hours a day in a split shift which revolves around the meal trains. When you are not serving customers, you will polish the silver, keep your station spotless, and help prepare for the next meal rush."

Smoothing her skirt, Miss Stewart wore a look of pride. "Our customers come from all walks of life. Railway passengers and railroad men as well as ranchers and business men. Should you spill something on your uniform, you must change immediately. One never knows when the young Mr. Harvey will conduct a surprise inspection."

Katherine stole a glance at Eunice who stood ramrod straight, her eyes riveted on the house manager. Mom hadn't mentioned the rigid rules. Was the job this regimented when she worked for the company?

"You may not wear make-up or jewelry, and your hair is to be worn in a bun at the nape of your neck. There is to be absolutely no chewing gum. Now, follow me, and I will show you where you are to take your meals. We have an employee dining room that serves the staff."

A sobbing woman ran past the doorway. Moments later, a door slammed deep in the house. Katherine bit her lip. What was that about?

Miss Stewart peered at her. "Miss Newman, are you listening?"

"Uh, yes, ma'am. But shouldn't you see to that young woman? She's crying."

"She has been dismissed and disagrees with our decision." She sighed. "Not everyone is Harvey Girl material, Miss Newman. Our rules are meant to be followed to the letter. Is that understood?"

Nodding, Katherine wiped damp palms on her skirt. Was she Harvey Girl material?

Katherine opened her eyes and squinted at the bright sunshine pouring into the bedroom. She sat up and glanced at Eunice. "What time is it?" Katherine fumbled for her watch on the night stand.

"Nine o'clock."

Swinging her feet over the edge of the bed, Katherine yawned. "I never sleep this late." She opened the closet door and pulled out the uniform that had been delivered during their orientation. Laying it on her bed, she fingered the multiple layers of clothing.

"There is certainly more to this than meets the eye."

Eunice grinned. "Let me help you. With the amount of starch they use in these petticoats, they don't readily move of their own accord."

"I've got to figure this out on my own. Besides, you need to get dressed, too."

Katherine slipped behind the privacy screen in the corner. "By the time we find our way to the cafeteria, we'll only have time for toast and juice."

"Hopefully we'll get faster at putting on our uniforms. Otherwise, we're going to starve."

The girls rushed to the employee dining room and bolted down their breakfast. After taking their soiled dishes to the kitchen, Katherine and Eunice hurried to the dining room as the ornate clock on the wall began to strike the hour. The dozen women in the room stared at them as one. A woman dressed in white approached. She appeared to be in her mid-fifties. "Hello, girls. I'm Miss Washington. I assume you are Miss Newman and Miss Holland."

"Yes, ma'm. I'm Katherine Newman, and this is my friend Eunice Holland."

"How do you do, Miss Washington," Eunice whispered.

"In the future, please arrive a few minutes prior to your shift start time. Here are your badges. Please pin them onto your apron. After I make today's assignments, I will familiarize you with our system. You will be responsible for a small section of tables until you prove your ability to perform satisfactorily. Once we determine you are eligible to stay, your sections will be the same as everyone else's. Understood?"

Katherine nodded. Now she knew how her cousin felt when he joined the army.

Miss Washington cleared her throat, and the noise ceased. She gestured to Katherine and Eunice. "This is Miss Newman and Miss Holland. Please make them welcome." A smattering of applause sounded after which Miss Washington issued tasks and information from her clip board in clipped sentences.

Dismissing the staff, she turned to Katherine and Eunice. "Miss Stewart explained our policies and how to conduct yourselves while employed by the Harvey Company. It is my responsibility to train you to be the best Harvey girls possible. The information you must absorb is vast, so do not hesitate to ask questions. I would rather have you ask questions and do something correctly than risk figuring it out on your own."

She led them into the lunch room. A horse-shoe shaped counter took up one corner. In the center of the room, tables were covered in white cloths identical to the dining room. "You ladies will work here. It's a more casual environment and not as fast paced because we don't serve as many courses."

Katherine took a deep breath. Miss Washington seemed anxious for her to succeed. Maybe she could do this after all.

"The rush begins when we hear the train. The first course is either fruit or salad and is plated as soon as we hear the whistle. When the vehicle pulls into the depot, a gong is sounded by one of the bus boys, and the passengers are ushered into the House where they are directed to either the dining room or the lunch room. Gentlemen are required to wear jackets in the dining room but not the lunch room."

Pointing to the station near the counter, Miss Washington said, "You must stand silently at your station until customers are seated. The beverage girl will ask each person what they care to drink and indicate their choice by arranging the cup in a precise position. I've written the code on these cards. Memorize them. A cup right side up in its saucer means coffee. Upside down means hot tea, and upside down but tilted against the saucer means iced tea. If the cup is upside down, away from the saucer it means milk."

"What a clever idea." Eunice smiled.

"The Harvey Company is well-known for its food and service. We serve the finest meals the United States has to offer. The Santa Fe provides ice cars that enable us to serve California cantaloupes, fresh whitefish, sage-fed quail, Texas beef, sea turtles and sea celery and blue point oysters on the half shell. We have English pea soup, roast sirloin of beef au jus, pork with applesauce, duck, ice cream, Edam and Roquefort cheese, and every fruit imaginable. We top off our meals with homemade pie cut into four servings instead of the traditional six."

Katherine patted her stomach.

"I know how you feel." Miss Washington beamed.

The shrill whistle pealed from an incoming train. Miss Washington clapped her hands. "All right, boys and girls, let's move!"

A procession of servers brought out the fruit plates and laid them at each place setting. Moments later, the crowd burst in the room and rushed for their seats.

Katherine gripped her order pad and straightened her shoulders. She could do this. Couldn't she?

A week later, Katherine made her way to the lunch room to await Miss Washington's arrival with the staff assignments and information for the day. The head waitress breezed into the room and clapped her hands to get everyone's attention. "Before I begin, I'd like to say that both Eunice Holland and Katherine Newman have successfully completed their first week here at the Williams' Harvey House." The room erupted in cheering. "Effective immediately, they will both be assigned a full section to serve. Congratulations."

Katherine grinned and ducked her head. She'd passed the first hurdle.

During her break, Miss Washington pulled Katherine aside. "I noticed how kind you were to Sally Thornton. You pointed out an error she made and coached her how to perform correctly while allowing her to maintain her dignity. I'm impressed, Miss Newman. Keep up the good work, and you'll go far in the Harvey Company."

"Thank you, Miss Washington." Perhaps leaving her teaching job in Warren had been a good idea after all. Turning, Katherine gathered her order pad from the counter and glanced at the server at the coffee station. The girl sneered at Katherine before bending to retrieve a tray of cups from the cabinet. Katherine's eyes widened. What had she done to offend the girl?

A train whistle shrieked in the distance, and the room came alive with activity. Katherine hurried to her section and risked another glance at the coffee station.

Vacant.

Releasing a pent-up sigh, Katherine waited for the surge of customers. *What is the girl's name? Patsy? Patricia? Pamela. That's it. How could she be angry at Katherine, they barely knew each other.*

The dining room filled quickly, and she approached a table where a portly man with mutton-chop whiskers perused the menu.

"What would you like, sir?"

"I'll have the Manhattan Clam Chowder followed by the Roast Sugar Cured Ham Sandwich. I love Harvey House ham."

"Would you care for any dessert?"

Patting his rotund belly, he laughed. "Absolutely. I'll take a slice of your gooseberry pie."

"Coming right up. Enjoy your fruit." Katherine moved to her next table. Moments later she had collected all the orders from her section, and she pivoted toward the kitchen.

Pamela barreled into Katherine's shoulder, and the tray in her arms crashed to the floor. Cups shattered, and dark brown liquid splattered the length of Katherine's apron.

"Look what you made me do. Why don't you pay more attention? You're so clumsy." The girl's strident voice filled the silent dining hall.

Perspiration broke out on Katherine's forehead. Where had Pamela come from?

"I—"

"Well, aren't you going to help me clean up this mess?"

Miss Washington rushed to them, a bus boy at her side. She leaned over the two women and spoke through clenched teeth. "Miss Keene, keep your voice down, and Miss Newman, go change your uniform. I will cover your section until you return."

Tears filled Katherine's eyes. The accident wasn't her fault. Did Miss Washington recognize that? "I'm sorry."

"No time for apologies, Miss Newman. We'll discuss this later. Go change and be quick about it."

Katherine climbed to her feet and hurried toward the door. She glanced over her shoulder and gasped. Pamela smirked at her from the center of the room.

Had the girl caused the scene on purpose? If so, what else did she have in mind to torment her?

Chapter Five

Katherine tucked her skirt around her legs and lowered herself onto the wooden chaise lounge behind the restaurant. Eunice reclined in the rope hammock under a straggly pinyon pine. Her nose was buried in L. Frank Baum's latest, *The Emerald City of Oz.*

She looked at Katherine and smiled. "Nice to be able to sit outside again, isn't it?"

"Who knew a fire in Idaho and Montana could affect us here in Arizona."

"They say smoke could be seen all the way to western New York."

"If it weren't for the rains, the fire might still be burning." Katherine shuddered.

"It's being called the Idaho Big Burn."

"I thought you'd take advantage of the clear weather and head to the Grand Canyon with some of the others."

"I love sitting on the rim and watching the colors change as the sun moves through the canyon, but the idea of a long car ride didn't appeal to me. In the four months since becoming a Harvey Girl, I've traveled more than I ever did in my whole life." She brushed an errant strand of hair away from her face. "At least the sizzling days are finally giving way to cool breezes. Not sure how much more of the heat I can take."

"Doesn't it get warm in Ohio?"

"Not like this. Even during our hottest summers, the temperatures drop at night."

A bald eagle swooped and danced on the thermals above her head. "I've also seen more birds and animals than I ever thought possible. Not that I'm a city girl, but Warren isn't exactly teeming with wildlife."

"I could do without the insect population." Eunice shuddered. "When I shook my shoes yesterday, some creepy-crawly the size of a fifty-cent piece fell out. I will never get used to that."

"Me either. Maybe we can go to Flagstaff on our next day off. Their bugs don't seem as fierce." Katherine held up her letter-writing materials. "It's been days since I last wrote to my family. They're going to think I'm lost in the desert."

Eunice giggled. "Or attacked by over-sized insects."

Katherine chuckled and pulled a sheet of stationery from the box. Setting the bottle of ink on the arm of the chair, she unscrewed the lid from her pen. She dipped the implement and began to write.

Dear Mom and Dad:

You would not recognize your daughter. I'm as brown as a walnut from all the sunshine we get here. I almost never remember to wear my hat. Despite being the end of October, it's still quite warm.

As I write Eunice is lying in one of the hammocks pretending to read, but her eyes are closed more than they are open. I don't blame her. The work we do is very demanding. We are on our feet during our entire shift, lifting and carrying stacks of dishware. I love my job and only miss the students a little bit.

The challenge of recalling the daily specials and training new girls keeps me on my toes. My time here has made me realize I have value, and just because Henry was foolish enough to decide he doesn't love me, doesn't change that. Eunice tells me there are plenty of other fish in the sea. (Or as she says, railroad men on the trains.) I told her things are fine just the way they are, but she has her eye on one of the cooks. He hasn't gotten the nerve up to ask Miss Washington if they can date. Maybe by Christmas.

We've had a couple of interesting days this week. First, Mr. Harvey showed up on Monday totally unannounced. Miss Washington was fit to be tied. We all stood at our stations while he dusted his handkerchief across every surface in the room. He even went into the storage closet and examined the plates for chips. About the time we thought he was satisfied, he overturned a table he said was improperly set. I thought Miss Washington was going to faint. She takes great pride in running the house to exacting standards. She and Mr. Harvey were in her office for nearly an hour.

"Don't forget to tell your folks about the mayonnaise debacle."

Katherine squinted at Eunice. "Did the poor boy need to be fired?"

Eunice shrugged. "Apparently we take our condiments seriously, and rat poison is not an acceptable ingredient."

"Do you think he did it on purpose? The cook threatened to call the police if he didn't leave immediately."

"The way he high-tailed it out of the restaurant makes me wonder, but Cook told me later he thinks the boy isn't very smart."

"Why would the man have dangerous chemicals in the kitchen, anyway?"

"He's an odd duck. Why does he do anything he does?"

"Miss Stewart insisted he mark the container in huge, red letters and lock it in the storage shed."

Eunice dropped her gaze to the book, and Katherine returned to her letter.

In two weeks, I begin my stint on night shift. Some of the girls say it's easier because there are fewer passengers who get off the trains at night. I'm not sure how I will adjust to sleeping during the day, although I guess if I'm tired enough anything is possible.

I'm over halfway through my six-month contract and have decided to sign on again if the Company wants me. I'll be home after Christmas, complements of the Company. I've become an experienced train rider, hardly noticing the motion any more.

How are things at home?

Home. Katherine nibbled on the end of her pen. Would she ever stop thinking about Henry when her thoughts turned toward Warren? What was he doing? Did he miss her, or was he happy and feeling free since walking away from her? Was he seeing someone else? Perhaps Lucy Flowers. She always had eyes for Henry. Were the two of them ambling through town, Henry's crystal blue eyes smiling down on Lucy, her hand tucked in the crook of his elbow? His silvery-blond hair ruffling in the breeze and his suit impeccably washed and pressed as they window-shopped.

"Stop."

Katherine turned toward Eunice. "What?"

"Stop daydreaming about Henry."

"How did you know—"

"Because you get this goofy, dreamy-eyed look on your face, and you sigh with every breath. Forget about Henry. You can do better than him."

"I know, but—"

"Sorry to keep interrupting, but listen to me. You have a new life here. You will meet someone else, fall madly in love, and ride off into the sunset." She grinned. "Or at least the tumbleweeds."

"You're a good friend, Eunice."

Eunice puffed out her chest. "Of course, I am. The best."

Katherine rubbed her forehead. Would she ever be able to put Henry behind her?

The ever-present sun beat down on Katherine as she climbed the steps into the Emporium. Not that she missed the biting, Ohio winters, but it didn't feel like Christmas was on its way without a nip in the air and white, fluffy snow on the ground.

Because she started working nights the following day, she could no longer put off purchasing her family's gifts. As it was, the items would probably arrive late at her parents' home. She glanced around the large store. Packing their shop with an extensive selection of items, the proprietors, Mr. and Mrs. Lambert, took great pride in their ability to keep all the newest inventions and frivolities stocked.

A display of gloves caught her attention, and she wandered to the rack. The kid gloves were as soft as butter. Her mother would like the tan pair. Stroking the supple leather, Katherine spied a glass case filled with jewelry and watches. Would her mother prefer something sparkly? Shrugging, she wandered to a shelf of cookbooks. Why couldn't she get into the holiday spirit?

She caught sight of herself in the mirror. Dark shadows hung below her eyes, and she grimaced at her image. You know exactly why you're blue, Katherine Newman. You thought you'd be planning a wedding, and instead you're waiting tables in the desert.

The front door of the emporium burst open, and Eunice barreled in with three of the girls from work. Eunice waved from the doorway. "Katherine! Are you finished in here? We've decided to take a road trip, and it won't be complete without you."

"Where did you get a car?"

"Betty's boyfriend has an Oldsmobile that's a real beater, but it should get us where we're going. He's letting her borrow it while he's out of town."

"Betty's boyfriend?" Katherine rolled her eyes. She sounded like a parrot.

Eunice walked to where Katherine stood. "Come on, we'll explain everything in the car. We need to leave now if we're going to make curfew."

Katherine nibbled her lower lip then shook her head. "I haven't bought a single Christmas gift. I should stay here."

"You can shop in Flagstaff. Some of the larger stores will even ship your purchases for you. Now, come on. You're running out of excuses." Eunice beamed. "And it might be just the ticket to help you cheer up."

"Cheer up?" Good grief, she was repeating Eunice's words again.

"You're putting on a good show, but I know you're still upset about this Henry fellow. A change of scenery will do you good." She hugged Katherine. "I won't take no for an answer."

"Then I guess I'm ready to go."

Eunice giggled and handed Katherine her shawl. "I brought this for you in case we don't get back before dark. The nights get chilly once the sun goes down."

"You really weren't going to take no, were you?"

Eunice gave her a sidelong glance as the girls trooped out of the store to the car parked out front. They crawled into the vehicle, and Betty turned west on Route 40.

"Is anyone going to give me the scoop about Betty here and her imaginary boyfriend who owns this fabulous car?" Katherine shouted above the roar of the engine.

The other girls burst out laughing. Regina Ortlesby gave Katherine a good-natured poke. "If you weren't such a workaholic, you'd know. She's been seeing Phil Green from down at the bank. It was love at first sight when he cashed one of her checks."

Katherine grinned. "Good choice, Betty. He's a looker. But does Miss Washington know about him?"

"Not yet."

Two of the girls exchanged a knowing glance. "It will be all over if she finds out. You know what the handbook says about dating."

Katherine's heart tugged. She hadn't bothered to read that section of the manual.

The vehicle bumped and swayed on the hard-packed dirt road, and Betty turned off the highway into the town and drove down Main Street.

"Pull in over there at the Crater Café, Betty. Susan Higgins told me it's a great place to eat," Regina pointed to a small building at the end of the street. Betty parked the car, and they hurried into the restaurant. Seated at a booth by the window, they could see the majestic peaks of Mt. Humphreys.

"I never tire looking at that beautiful view," murmured Katherine. The others nodded in agreement.

The waitress approached their table, and they ordered lunch. She tucked the pencil in her bedraggled bun at the base of her neck. "Have you heard the news? Congress finally caved in and agreed we could write a constitution. The Constitutional Convention will convene tomorrow to get started." She grinned. "Arizona might get statehood yet."

Katherine leaned forward. "How exciting. I heard New Mexico also petitioned to become a state."

"We'll just have to see who wins the race." The woman picked up their menus and headed to the kitchen.

Their food arrived quickly, and the women dug in while discussing the waitress's announcement.

"No dawdling, ladies. There's lots to see before the day is done," Regina said. "I'll take care of bill, and we can settle up later."

"You're feeling flush," Betty said.

Regina shrugged. "With the company covering our room and board, there's little need to spend."

The women finished their meal and left the small establishment. They piled into the car while Betty studied the map. "Which way to the park, girls? Phil always drives, so I'm not sure where to go."

Looking over Betty's shoulder at the paper, Pauline said, "There it is." She gestured to the small words indicating the location of the attraction. "I'll navigate."

After a short drive, the girls arrived at the park and went inside the visitor center to view the exhibits. An hour later, they walked out of the small building to one of the trailheads behind the Center. They took turns pointing out interesting flora and reading from the plaques posted at various locations along the trail.

"I had no idea there were volcanoes here in America." Regina blotted at her face with a lace-trimmed handkerchief. "This is fascinating."

The women wandered and chatted among themselves as the sun slipped toward the horizon.

Katherine admired the scarlet and orange streaks of the setting sun then gasped.

"Girls, the sun is almost down. What time is it?"

Betty looked at her watch. "Oh, no. We should have left an hour ago. We're going to miss curfew."

Rushing to the car, they left the park. Betty drove back into Flagstaff, making several turns along the way.

Regina leaned forward. "Betty, do know where we are? We should have seen the signs for Route 40 by now."

Betty pulled over and snatched the map from Pauline. "I thought you were navigating."

"And I thought you knew what you were doing."

Betty put her hands over her face and began to cry. "Apparently, I don't. I'm sorry, girls. It will be my fault if we get caught and fired."

Regina stroked Betty's shoulder. "We're in this together. Besides, I've lost count of the number of times the cook has let me in after hours."

Pauline studied the map, then smiled. "It's okay, Betty. We're not that far off track. If you turn right at the end of this street and then make the next left, we should see Route 40."

Guiding the car back onto the road, Betty soon had them heading back toward Williams. After she parked the vehicle, the girls climbed out and tiptoed around the back of the building to the kitchen. Regina scratched at the door. "Psssst, John. It's me, Regina."

The girls heard footsteps before the door opened a crack. John peered out into the dark. "Who?"

"Regina. And I've got three of the other girls with me. We got lost in Flagstaff. Can you let us in?"

"Don't I always? Just be quiet as you sneak upstairs, and I won't report you."

The girls removed their shoes and lifted their skirts. They crept through the building and headed toward the stairs.

Pauline gasped, and the foursome stopped short. Miss Washington stood on the landing, arms crossed and a deep frown on her face.

Chapter Six:

"Would you please accompany me to my office, Miss Newman?" Miss Stewart beckoned to Katherine after the shift announcements were complete.

Katherine's palms moistened. A month had passed since she and the others had broken curfew. They had been reprimanded for their tardiness and cautioned not to be late in the future. That seemed to be the end of it, but perhaps Miss Stewart was unhappy with some aspect of her performance.

"Certainly, Miss Stewart." Katherine's stomach quivered as she followed the head waitress down the corridor.

They walked in silence to Miss Stewart's cubby sized office. Miss Washington stood by the desk her face unreadable.

Katherine swallowed past the lump in her throat. "Good morning." She had minimal contact with the House Manager, and it was usually to carry messages or a meal to her. What terrible infraction had she committed to be subjected to a meeting with her?

"Please sit down, Miss Newman. This will only take a moment." Miss Washington pointed to a chair tucked in the corner of the room.

Beads of perspiration formed on Katherine's upper lip, and she stifled the impulse to wipe them away. Seating herself, she clasped her hands in her lap and tried to look nonchalant.

"Miss Newman, we have an offer we would like you to consider. Miss Stewart will be leaving on Friday to care for her mother who is gravely ill. Despite last month's curfew violation, we have been impressed with your performance. We'd like you to accept the position of Head Waitress."

"What?" Katherine gaped at the two women.

"We'd like to promote you to Head Waitress. We have monitored your progress and find you to be an excellent candidate. You have leadership qualities, and the girls seem to like you. There are three women who should be ahead of you for consideration. One of them has indicated she will not be renewing her contract, and the other two are not up to the task. They are good waitresses, but not the caliber individual we look for in management."

"You want me?" She licked her dry lips.

Miss Washington nodded, a smile finally appearing on her face. "Will you consider the opportunity and let us know by tomorrow before the morning announcements? We understand it is short notice, but if you decide not to accept, we will need to contact the other Harvey Houses to determine if there are suitable candidates elsewhere."

"Thank you! I will think about this and meet you in here prior to the staff gathering. I am honored to have been chosen."

Rushing to the dining room, Katherine arrived as the first wave of patrons entered. She pulled her order pad from her pocket and lined up next to Eunice. On her right, Pamela jabbed her with her elbow and scowled. "Do you have to stand so close?"

Katherine released an exasperated sigh. Would she ever get used to Pamela's prickly personality? She'd have to if she accepted the position of Head Waitress. Did she have what it took to do the job?

The next morning dawned brightly as if celebrating Katherine's news. She bounded down the stairs and nearly knocked over one of the maintenance men who was tightening a spindle on the banister.

"Sorry, Mr. Brendan."

"Watch yourself, missy. Work won't go well today if you're a bull in the china shop!"

"Right you are!"

She stopped in front of Miss Stewart's office and knocked.

"Enter!"

Katherine opened the door and stepped inside. Miss Washington occupied the same corner of the office she had the night before, and Miss Stewart sat behind the desk. Clearing her throat, Katherine tucked her hands into the pockets of her skirt. "I'd like to accept the position of Head Waitress. That is if you still want me."

Miss Washington beamed. "Of course, we still want you. I'll make the announcement this morning and split up your station among the women, so you may begin training immediately." She gestured to a stack of paper on her desk. "Because you are taking a different position, you will be offered a new contract. Unfortunately, you will miss the sabbatical normally given between assignments, but we can make arrangements for you to take a few days off. Congratulations, Miss Newman."

The three women went to the dining room where the next shift of girls congregated, and Miss Washington clapped her hands. Conversation ceased. "I have good news and bad news. The bad news is that we are losing Miss Stewart who must go home to tend to her ailing mother, but the good news is that Miss Newman has accepted our offer to take her place as Head Waitress."

Applause erupted, and Katherine's face warmed. From her usual position at the coffee station, Pamela glared at Katherine.

Katherine's eyes widened at the woman's malevolent look. What had she done to earn the woman's rancor? Would she make work difficult now that Katherine was her supervisor?

"Can you believe they promoted Katherine Newman of all people?"

Katherine froze on the landing. Whispered voices filtered toward her from the bottom of the stairs.

"It doesn't really surprise me. Her hoity-toity attitude must have impressed Miss Stewart."

"She's not going to be able to handle the job. Waiting tables is one thing, but there's so much more to head waitress job."

"Weren't you next in line? You've been working here longer. You should have been selected."

"Miss Washington told me that even though I was next in line Katherine was a better fit. Whatever that means." Sarcasm dripped from the woman's voice.

"What are you going to do?"

"Something to make her look bad, but I have to figure out how to do it so no one suspects me."

"I've got some ideas."

Katherine's heart pounded. She needed to confront the women. If she was going to be Head Waitress, she had to conduct herself with authority. She took a deep breath and descended the stairs on silent feet. Hopefully the women wouldn't sense her terror.

"Excellent—"

"If you don't want to get caught talking about someone behind her back, you might want to have your conversation in a less public area." Katherine stood on the bottom step above the conspirators.

Pamela blanched, and Connie's mouth formed a perfect O.

Squaring her shoulders, Katherine looked down at the pair. "I won't discuss this with Miss Washington, but I suggest you change your plans to undermine me. That kind of behavior will get you fired."

Connie nodded her face blotched with red spots.

Pamela held Katherine's gaze and raised her chin. "Talk to Miss Washington all you want. It will be your word against mine." She tugged on Connie's arm. "Come on, Connie. There's nothing left to be said." Turning on her heel, she stalked away.

Katherine blew out a deep breath. Life was about to get harder.

Chapter Seven

Katherine laced her fingers together and straightened her spine. "You've been caught stealing, Pamela. I have to dismiss you."

Pamela's lip curled in a snarl. "I can't believe you're firing me. You think you're so much better than everyone else. I should have been promoted to Head Waitress last month, not you."

Sighing, Katherine gestured to the town deputy who stood behind the accused woman. "I'm sorry you feel that way, but the company has specific policies. We've decided not to press charges, but you must leave the premises immediately. Deputy Bradley will escort you to the train station, and your trunk will be sent over when Miss Washington has finished packing it."

Deputy Bradley gestured to the open door, and Pamela jumped to her feet, pointing her finger at Katherine. "You won't get away with this. My father is one of the most powerful men in Arizona. He could own this pathetic company. You just wait. I'll be sitting in that chair instead of you."

"That's enough." The deputy's face darkened, and he grabbed Pamela's upper arm, guiding her from the room. Pamela's screeching voice faded, and a door slammed deep within the building.

Katherine sagged against the back of her chair. "Well, that was uncomfortable. With any luck, that's the worst of my day." Her gaze fell on the overflowing basket of mail, and she plucked the top piece of paper from the stack.

"The list of new hires." She grimaced. "We'll need one more than anticipated. Hopefully..." Her eyes pierced the page, and her fingers gripped the stationery. Alice Jorgenson headed the roster of employees assigned to the Williams facility. Tossing the paper on her desk, Katherine rose and moved to the window. Staring out across the dusty expanse, she rubbed the back of her neck. Could she work with Alice? Was it possible to make a request for Alice to be posted elsewhere? What reason would Katherine give for making the request?

She shook her head. Miss Washington would expect her to be a professional. Alice would come, and Katherine would have to make the best of it. How would Alice feel when she realized Katherine was her boss? Her eyes narrowed. Did Alice know she was here? She couldn't possibly. It was simply a coincidence. A despicable coincidence.

Alice would room with Eunice who had lost three roommates in as many months.

What would Eunice think of the situation? Maybe it was for the best. Her friend could keep an eye on Henry's sister. Better to let Eunice know now, before Alice and her bags arrived.

Casting a final glance at the stark landscape, Katherine turned and walked to the door. Yanking it open, she jumped. Miss Washington stood in the doorway her hand raised as if to knock.

"Goodness, I never heard your footsteps!" Katherine pressed a hand against her throat.

"I was passing by and saw your light. Do you plan to retire shortly? Tomorrow will be a long day because new employees are arriving."

"I was coming to find you to discuss that very topic." She stepped back. "Please come in, this could take a while."

Miss Washington sat in the upholstered side chair tucked in the corner of Katherine's office. "You have a problem with the list."

"Not the list, just one particular person. Alice Jorgensen, Henry's sister."

"He's-the-reason-you're-a-Harvey-Girl-Henry?"

"One and the same."

"Well, I can see why you're a bit anxious over her arrival. How did she treat you after your break up with Henry?"

"I never let her get close enough before I left to find out. She must have been in on it or she would have kept in touch with me."

Miss Washington's forehead wrinkled. "Not necessarily, Katherine. She may have been embarrassed by what he did or think that you didn't want to speak with her. There are many reasons for her lack of contact. You should allow her to share her side of the story."

Katherine's face warmed. Miss Washington must think she was acting like a schoolgirl. Maybe she regretted promoting her.

Miss Washington patted Katherine's arm. "You haven't been prone to emotional decisions. Don't start now. It will be the death of you." She grinned. "Besides, you were here first, and I can always have her transferred somewhere else if it doesn't work out."

"You can do that?"

"Absolutely, but I'd rather not. Good help is difficult to find, and if she's a productive worker I'd rather not lose her because of personal differences with my head waitress. Think you can make this work?"

Katherine pressed her lips together and nodded. She would have to make this work, or the Jorgensen family would ruin her life a second time.

The following morning, Katherine avoided Alice's gaze and announced the new staff members. In a clipped voice, she gave out employee assignments then dismissed the gathering before marching back to her office. Once inside she tallied inventory, approved invoices, and created supply lists.

After three hours of handling paperwork, her eyes burned. She dropped her pencil on the desk and scrubbed at her face with cold fingers. She couldn't hide in her office during Alice's entire contract period. Confronting Henry's sister should be done sooner rather than later.

She pushed her self away from the desk. A knock sounded, and Katherine opened the door. Alice stood in the hallway.

Katherine frowned. "What are you doing away from the dining hall?"

"I'm on break." Alice's lower lip trembled. "You barely looked at me this morning, Katherine. I understand you're hurt, but why are you taking out your anger on me?"

"Come in. I'd rather not discuss this in the corridor." Katherine shut the door with a loud click.

Alice seated herself. "I didn't know you were here. Your parents haven't been very forthcoming about your location."

"Why should they? The town had plenty of fodder for gossip before I left. There's no reason to give them additional information."

"I understand."

"Do you?" Katherine took a deep breath. Professional. She promised Miss Washington, she'd be professional. "I didn't know you were arriving until yesterday, and quite frankly, I'm not sure how I feel about it. I've managed to make a life for myself here and am quite content. I miss my parents but very little else about Warren."

She crossed her arms. "I don't wish to discuss the past other than to say that Henry's behavior of leading me on for nearly a year before breaking off our relationship was abhorrent. And your family's complicit acceptance of the situation was no better. I thought you and I were friends, yet you did nothing to warn me or visit to see how I fared."

Katherine lifted her chin. "I cannot treat you any differently than I treat the other employees. Our past relationship means nothing here. Do you understand?"

Alice nodded her eyes moist. "Have you totally forgotten our friendship...the friendship you had with my family?"

"If you'll recall, Alice, your brother dumped me like a hot potato. Everywhere I turned, women stared at me or cut off the conversations they were obviously having about me. That got rather tiresome. My parents and I decided a fresh start somewhere else would be good for me." She stuffed her hands into her apron pockets. "It has been the right change. I've progressed through the ranks here and receive an excellent salary. I am my own person. I don't need others to ensure my happiness."

Alice leaned forward. "I'm sorry for what Henry did. It was inexcusable no matter what his reasons. The family didn't talk to him for days. Then we realized he was just as miserable as we were."

"Why on earth would he be miserable? It was his idea."

"Do you really want to hear this, Katherine?"

"I suppose I must at some point. Especially if we are going to work together."

"First of all, whether you believe me or not, Henry still loves you very much. He never felt good enough for you. He used to tell me how lucky he was that you were his girl. He couldn't believe it when you said yes after he had summoned up the courage to ask you out. Anyway, that's why he broke up with you."

"He broke my heart because he thinks I'm too good for him? You're right. I find that hard to believe."

"Henry is not as confident as he appears, Katherine. He has always felt you were smarter than he is. His friends ribbed him terribly about marrying up when he started courting you. Then when things started getting tight at the farm, he began to feel like he couldn't offer you the security a man should when he takes a woman as his wife. A few weeks later, we found out things were worse than we thought. Mr. Brown showed up to tell us that Mr. Swenson was calling in our loan. My father had only been making the interest payments for months, and I guess Mr. Swenson decided that had gone on long enough. We managed to get an extension, but the bottom line is if we can't pay him the back money we owe as well as the current principal and interest payments by June we're going to lose the farm."

"Is that why you're here? Will you be sending your paycheck home?"

"Yes," whispered Alice brokenly.

"I'm sorry to hear that. The farm has been your father's life. But you need to understand my side of things, Alice. I thought Henry and I had an honest and open relationship. If two people are going to be soul mates in marriage, the partners can't pick and choose what they are going to share with each other. If Henry thought I would love him less because of his financial situation, he must believe me to be quite shallow. For those reasons, I've come to realize it's a good thing we didn't marry."

"But Henry still loves you." Tears coursed down Alice's cheeks.

"It's obviously a conditional type of love, and that's not good enough for me." She opened the door to her office. "End of discussion. I appreciate your candor, Alice. But we will not speak of this again. For the time being, let's keep our conversations on professional topics only. Is that clear?"

"Quite clear. You certainly have changed, Katherine, and I'm not sure it's for the better." Alice's lips thinned, and she walked out.

Katherine closed the door and dropped into the chair, biting back her sobs.

Chapter Eight

A week later, Katherine languished on her bed. Enjoying her first day off in more than ten days, she propped herself against the pillow and opened her book. The curtain fluttered in the breeze wafting through the window. Sighing, she took a deep breath.

She froze and sniffed the air.

Smoke?

Sliding a bookmark between the pages, she laid the volume on her nightstand and took another breath. The acrid smell of burning wood filled her nostrils. Katherine jumped to her feet and raised the casement, her hands trembling. Poking her head outside, she looked back and forth searching for flames.

Nothing.

Had Cook scorched something in the kitchen? Perhaps one of the boys was building a bonfire.

She shook her head. What was she thinking? Constructed entirely of wood, the tiny town of Williams was a collection of kindling. No one built a fire on purpose, and certainly not a bonfire.

From deep inside the house, someone shouted.

Then screamed.

Katherine yanked her head inside and turned toward the door. Gray smoke curled into the room from under the door.

Fire! The house was on fire.

She raced to the door, and with a fingertip touched the doorknob. Warm, but not scalding. Should she go out the window? The other girls. Who was upstairs? Was anyone asleep? She must evacuate them from the building. Grabbing a blouse from the closet, she shoved it into the pitcher of water on her dresser. She wrung out the fabric until it no longer dripped, rolled it, and tied it around her nose and mouth. She cracked the door and peeked into the corridor. Clouds of smoke obscured her vision. Blinking away the grit from her eyes, she waved her arms to clear a path. The haze swirled around her head, and the sharp odor pierced her lungs. Stumbling, she fell to one knee as a paroxysm of coughing overtook her.

Must. Get. Out.

Her eyes weeping tears of pain, she crawled forward and stretched out her hand in front of herself then to the side. Where was the wall?

Reaching. Reaching.

Her fingers brushed the papered surface, and a sob caught in her throat. She could follow the corridor to the stairs and escape. Rising to a crouch, she fisted her hand and banged on the wall as she made her way toward the stairs.

A door to her right opened, and two girls in dressing gowns appeared through the smoke. Crying, they clung to each other.

Katherine peered at them through swollen eyes. She grabbed the hand of the closest girl, and the pair fell to the floor beside her. "Stay low and follow me."

They nodded, and she led them forward continuing to bang on the wall as they went. At each room, she stopped and pushed open the door.

From downstairs, shouting and screaming punctuated the fetid air. In the distance, a bell clanged. Her chest tightened. Pealing madly, the alarm called out to the volunteer firemen.

Would help arrive before they all perished?

Katherine sat on a crate, a blanket draped around her shoulders. Coughing, she sipped water from the chipped teacup someone had salvaged. Men and women in various states of dress stared at the charred shell of the kitchen with glazed eyes sunken in soot-smudged faces.

She shuddered and hunched her shoulders. She almost died. Overcome with smoke, she and the other girls had become disoriented and failed to find the stairs. If one of the firemen hadn't climbed to the second floor, they all would have succumbed. A tragic casualty of a foolish accident.

Rubbing her chest, she winced. Each breath burned her throat and lungs. Draining the last of the water, she climbed to her feet. She was getting morbid, and the others needed help more than she did. Fortunately, the entire staff had managed to abandon the building, and there were no serious injuries.

Miss Washington beckoned to her from beside the fire chief. Katherine pulled the blanket tighter and limped to them.

She swallowed and grimaced. "What seems to be the cause of the blaze, sir?" Her voice sounded raspy and weak.

The fire chief squinted toward the blackened frame. "There was a grease spill at the stove. The kitchen is gutted, and there is extensive water and smoke damage to the rest of the building. You won't be operating for a while."

Nodding at him, she tried not to cry.

No restaurant meant no job. Now what?

Chapter Nine

Henry stared into the fire and clutched the letter from Alice. He read again the words that were burned into his brain.

Katherine Newman is the Head Waitress here. She's different from the girl we knew last year. Serious and professional to a fault, it's almost as if she's afraid to let down her guard. We spoke about you, Henry. She's angry, so very angry, but underneath I think she still loves you. You should come for a visit to surprise her. We have guest rooms where you could stay.

Henry pinched the bridge of his nose as he pondered the words: *I think she still loves you.* Was it true that Katherine still loved him? Was fate giving him a second chance to build a life with her?

Financial worries had prompted Alice to get a job. Then Alice was assigned to the same location as Katherine. What were the chances of that happening?

He shoved the letter into his pocket. Would Katherine be upset if he showed up unannounced? Surely, she'd understand he needed to apologize in person for the way he'd severed their relationship. If she would speak to him. What if he traveled all the way to Arizona, and she wouldn't see him? That's why he would have to surprise her.

He leapt from his chair and hurried to his room. Kneeling, Henry pulled his satchel from under the bed. He unzipped the bag then wrenched open the top drawer of his dresser.

"What am I doing?" Henry closed the drawer with a bang and dropped onto the bed. "I can't sashay off to Arizona as if I have no responsibilities. Every penny of my salary must go into the family coffer to pay the mortgage. To use some of that money for personal gain would be selfish."

"But a phone call might work."

Henry's head pivoted toward the voice. Dad stood in the doorway, a grin on his face. "You're a good son. The best any man could wish for, and I can't be selfish either. A phone call wouldn't be nearly as expensive as a train ride. Call Katherine. Make amends and ask her forgiveness. What happens after that is anybody's guess, but you'll have done the right thing."

"I don't know, Dad. What if she won't speak to me?"

"All you can do is try. Talk to Alice first, ask her to put in a good word for you."

Footsteps pounded up the stairs, and Carl's head popped from behind dad. "Henry, go to the general store. Alice is on the telephone for you. She has news about Katherine."

Henry gaped at his brother. The decision had been made for him.

Katherine stepped off the train in Williams. The House Manager in Winslow had offered her the Head Waitress job, but after two weeks of working with their staff, she knew it wasn't the job for her. When she received notification the renovations were complete in Williams, she couldn't pack her bag fast enough.

She crossed the tracks and made her way into the house. In the lobby, Alice knelt by the main staircase polishing the railing. She rushed toward Katherine, tucking the rag into her pocket. "It's good to have you back. May I take your bag upstairs so you can check in with Miss Washington?"

Katherine's shoulders stiffened. With all the Harvey House locations, why did Alice have to be assigned to Williams? She pasted a smile on her face. "That would be nice. Did anything exciting happen while I was away?"

"I spoke with Henry. He asked about you."

A chill swept over Katherine. "Why would Henry call? Is everything all right at home?"

"Everything is fine. I called him. One day I was so very homesick. You know how close our family is, and I get lonely. The girls are fun and have been kind to me, but it's not the same." She sniffled. "Anyway, he wants to apologize for hurting you. He was disappointed you were not here."

"Still trying to push us back together, Alice? I thought I made it clear that I wasn't interested in Henry."

"But he still loves you."

Katherine frowned. "I find that difficult to believe. He's the one who broke up with me. Besides, if he really wanted to apologize to me, he would come to Williams."

"You know he can't afford that." She tucked an envelope in Katherine's pocket. "He sent you a letter that explains everything. Please read it."

Katherine pointed her finger at Alice. "I don't want to tell you again. Stay out of my personal life. And do not mention Henry to me again, or I'll have you transferred. Or worse, fired." Luggage in hand, she stalked toward the House Manager's office, the envelope like a stone in her pocket.

Dear Katherine:

Alice says you are experiencing great success in your new career. I'm not surprised because you are creative and smart, able to make the most of any situation. The new school teacher has settled in, but the children haven't warmed up to her yet. She doesn't seem to have your ability to build relationships with them.

I could go on with more news from home, but I have stalled long enough. Besides, I have torn up so many drafts, I'm almost out of paper.

I'll say it simply, and I hope you believe my words are sincere. I don't deserve your forgiveness, but I am writing to ask for it anyway.

As if I needed reminding, Alice told me I hurt you. I know that, and I deeply regret my actions that brought you pain. You are a kind and gracious woman, deserving of all the happiness this life can bring. That I have injured you brings me shame.

Please, forgive this flawed and remorseful man.

Your humble servant,

Henry Jorgensen, Jr.

Katherine crumpled the letter and tossed it in the waste bin next to her desk. Heart pounding, she covered her face and sobbed.

Chapter Ten

Katherine dropped her pencil on the desk and massaged the stiffness from her shoulders. She pulled open the desk drawer, and her gaze fell on Henry's wrinkled letter.

After her crying spell when the missive arrived two weeks ago, she retrieved it from the trash can. It was a daily reminder of what she could have if she wanted it.

Sighing she rummaged through the clutter for an eraser. Too bad she couldn't erase her past. Who was she kidding? If she hated Henry as she claimed, why had she kept his letter?

A knock sounded on the door frame, and Eunice poked her head into the office.

"Here you are! I went to your room but couldn't find you!"

Katherine jumped and shut the drawer with a bang. "What's wrong?"

"Nothing. Everything is right! I can't wait to tell you all about it. You're going to be so excited. It's totally life-changing. I'm a new woman, and you can be, too."

Katherine smiled as Eunice's words tumbled over themselves. "Slow down and start from the beginning."

Eunice sank into one of the upholstered side chairs and took a deep breath. "Today was my day off. I was too tired to go hiking with the usual crowd, so I decided to go window shopping in town after lunch. I knew it wouldn't take too long, but the trip would get me out of the house for a while. I spent quite a bit of time at the Emporium. They have some new material and patterns to look at. I get so tired of wearing black I could scream."

Katherine raised an eyebrow. "You're in here because of a clothing emergency?"

"I'm not finished, yet."

"This is going to take a while, isn't it?"

"Ok, I'll skip to the end."

"You don't have to. However, you can drag out a story longer than any other woman here."

"Fine. While I was at the Emporium, I heard two ladies from town talking about a meeting at the church with some famous preacher man. You know I don't cotton much with religion, but I was desperate for something to do. Anyway, when I paid for my purchases, I asked Mrs. Lambert if she knew anything about the meeting, and she gave me a flyer." Eunice bounced in the chair. "I can't believe I hadn't heard about it. The town has supposedly been covered in leaflets about a bunch of revival meetings. I guess with the amount of time we spend working, there are a lot of things we miss."

Katherine crossed her arms. "Is this you skipping to the end?"

"Sorry. I'm wandering again. Where was I?" She tapped a finger on her chin. "Yes, the flyer. I had some extra time to kill while waiting for the meeting to begin, so I went to the church to watch them set up. While I was there, a very nice older gentleman sat with me, and we got to chatting. He asked me why I was there, and I showed him the notice. He seemed pleased to see it."

"When do you get to the point of the story?"

Eunice blushed. "I'm almost there. Anyway, we talked for a while, and then he left. Eventually it was time to begin and who should walk out onto the podium but the man I was speaking to. He was the revival preacher. He was such a nice man I listened to every word he said. He spoke about God which usually turns me off. But the way he talked about him was different than anything I had ever heard. The man said Jesus is God, and that He's our friend. Even when nothing is going our way, he carries our burdens."

Katherine rolled her eyes.

Eunice held up her hand. "That's what I used to think. But the preacher told us if we admitted we were sinners and asked Jesus to take away our sin, we would be new creatures. So, I did. And I am. A new creature, that is. I feel clean inside, Katherine. You have to experience it yourself to believe it."

"I'm happy for you, Eunice. You deserve a little happiness and comfort. I don't need God. I'm content with things as they are."

"There are meetings the rest of the week. Would you come with me to see for yourself before you discount what he is saying?"

"Thanks for the invitation. I'll think about it, but not now. It's late, and we need to turn in for the night." Katherine rose and hugged Eunice before gently ushering her out of the office. "Sleep tight, Eunice. I'll see you in the morning."

"G'night."

Katherine trudged up the stairs toward her quarters, nibbling her lower lip. Eunice was excited about her new found faith, and Katherine had given her the brush-off. A friend since the two of them arrived, Eunice deserved her support. But the last thing she needed was God. Her a sinner? Not likely. She wasn't like the convicts who dined at the house last week.

When the train pulled into the station, the girls remained in their rooms, and the male staff served the meals. Once the train and its prisoners departed, the women were allowed back into the room to clean up as normal.

She shuddered. Peeking through the kitchen door, she had watched the unkempt and unshaven men file into the dining room. Dirty and scowling, they barked at the servers and rattled their fetters. Banging spoons on the table they complained they needed forks and knives to eat. No one was foolish enough to grant that request.

After the meal, the felons formed a line, and the law enforcement officers searched them. Many a piece of Harvey silver was collected from the prisoners' pockets. One of the convicts took exception to being prodded and took a swing at his guard. The officer conked him on the head with the butt of his rifle, and the man crumpled to the floor. Two deputies dragged the unconscious man out the door, and the rest of the prisoners followed, mute and subdued.

Now, those were people who needed God. Not her.

Katherine pasted a smile on her face. "Are you ladies ready to go?" The day was gray and overcast. Why had she agreed to attend church with Eunice and some of the girls? A better idea would be to stay in bed and rest her aching feet.

Alice patted the cushion next to her. "There's room on the sofa. Would you like to sit down?"

"I'll wait in the lobby, if you don't mind. Thanks for the offer."

Blushing, Alice ducked her head.

Moments later, Eunice descended the stairs, and the group left the house.

Katherine hung back. Why had she been rude to Alice? The girl had reached out to her on numerous occasions, and Katherine snubbed her at every turn. She thought she had prepared herself for seeing Alice, but each time they passed in the dining room ugly feelings of betrayal reared up.

"I'm not a mean person, but I'm acting no better than Pamela did. This bitterness is exhausting. I need to put it aside." She grimaced. Easier said than done.

The group arrived at the church and selected a pew near the middle of the sanctuary. The room filled quickly, and the aisles were soon clogged with people. Word must have spread about the preacher.

The temperature in the crowded space escalated, and Katherine dabbed at the perspiration that had formed at her hairline. People continued to wedge themselves into the facility. Fathers held children on their shoulders, and mothers carried babies on their hips. The tangy odor of sweat hung in the warm, humid air.

Suddenly the noise ceased.

A man in his sixties or seventies strode onto the stage, followed by four other men who were at least a half foot taller than the guest of honor. He seemed to make up for his lack of height with a confident swagger and squared shoulders. An elderly woman was the last to seat herself on the stage.

"Beloved people, thank you for coming tonight. It's crowded and hot in here. Let the Word of God cool your bodies and your souls. Listen and learn." The man's voice carried to the far reaches of the sanctuary. He held up a large black book. "I'll be reading from the twenty-third chapter of Psalms.

"The Lord is my shepherd I shall not want. He maketh me lie down in green pastures. He leadeth me beside the still waters. He restoreth my soul; He leadeth me in the paths of righteousness for His name's sake. Yea, though I walk through the valley of the shadow of death, I will fear no evil; for Thou art with me; Thy rod and Thy staff they comfort me. Thou preparest a table before me in the presence of mine enemies; Thou anointest my head with oil; my cup runneth over. Surely goodness and mercy shall follow me all the days of my life; and I will dwell in the house of the Lord forever."

The man closed his Bible and peered over the metal rim of his glasses. He gripped the sides of the podium. "Who here is tired? Discouraged? Nursing a wounded heart?"

Katherine stiffened.

"Know this, beloved, people will let you down. People will hurt you, sometimes intentionally; sometimes not. People can be our best friends or our worst enemies. Occasionally it is the same person."

Katherine licked her dry lips. Was he looking at her?

"God is the same yesterday, today and tomorrow. He is our friend and our comforter. He is like a shepherd who takes care of his flock. Nothing is too much trouble for the shepherd. He wants His sheep fed, rested and cared for. That is what God does for us. We are too weak to carry our burdens alone. He will carry them for us if we let him.

"Life is hard. Each one of you works for a living; many of you work long days or multiple jobs. I am not saying that God will take away all of your problems, but rather He will be there with you to share the weight of them. He understands what we are experiencing. He sent His son, Jesus, who is also God, down to earth to be here with us.

"Jesus was tempted just as we are. He was tempted to be prideful and to do things on his own. He was also tempted to worship things other than God. We fall prey to these same issues. Each one of us can think of times when we let pride get the better of us. No matter what our station in life, we also worship things other than God – money, possessions, jobs; even other people. None of these things are eternal."

Katherine squirmed in her seat.

The preacher paused and surveyed the crowd. "'Surely goodness and mercy shall follow me all the days of my life; and I will dwell in the house of the Lord forever.' Beloved, God wants us to spend eternity with him. He wants us to dwell with him *forever*. All we have to do is ask Him, and He will be with us. Once He is in our hearts, He will accompany us through the dark places, our valleys. He will use His rod and staff to provide for us as the shepherd provides for His sheep. He will supply our needs which you should not confuse with our wants."

Laughter rumbled through the congregation.

"Yes, you know what I mean. We have lots of wants. God gives us what He knows is good for us. Our cup will run over. Think about what I have said tonight. Look deep into your heart and see where you stand. Are you prideful? Do you worship things rather than God, our Creator? Are you hurting? If you want someone to pray with you, please make your way to the front where these men and women will be standing. Come as we sing." He stepped away from the pulpit and bowed his head.

Through her tears, Katherine watched the man praying. She turned to Eunice who smiled and pointed to the altar. "God will take away your hurt, Katherine. Let's go talk with one of those men."

Dozens of people congregated at the base of the podium. Nodding, Katherine allowed Eunice to escort her down the aisle to the front of the room. The preacher beckoned to her then moved one of the chairs from the platform. She dropped into the hard, wooden chair and bowed her head.

The man kneeled in front of her, taking her balled fists into his hands. "Do you want to talk about it, my child? God is listening."

Katherine trembled. "Yes, I do." She dabbed at her eyes with a damp handkerchief. "I'm struggling to forgive friends who hurt me before I came to Arizona. But God can't forgive me until I release my anger. I would like to ask Him into my heart. Can you help me?"

"I would be honored to. Just bow your head, close your eyes, and repeat the words I say. God will hear you."

She nodded and repeated the preacher's words. "Dear Jesus, I'm a sinner, and I'm thankful You died for me. Please wash the darkness out of my heart and live inside me. Help me forgive my friends as You forgive me – completely. Amen."

Peace settled over her body, and she frowned. "What just happened? I'm light enough to float away on a cloud."

The pastor raised his hand in the air and grinned. "You're clean as a whistle. It's God inside you, child. He did just what you asked Him to. He shone His light into the corners of your heart and purged all that sin. You're a new person. Doesn't it feel good?"

"It does. I don't understand it."

"You don't have to understand, child. Just accept His gift."

Fresh tears coursed down Katherine's cheeks. The debilitating weight of bitterness was gone. Finally gone. She lunged forward and hugged the preacher, knocking his glasses askew.

Laughing, he extricated himself from her grasp. "Careful, child."

She turned toward the hand on her shoulder. "Eunice, I'm clean and new!"

"I'm so happy for you."

"Alice? Where is Alice? I must tell her. I've been awful to her."

A voice piped up from behind Eunice. "I'm here, Katherine, and I'm new, too!"

"Alice, can you ever forgive me? I've been hateful, and none of this was even your fault." Katherine embraced the young woman. Forgiving Alice was one thing, but what about Henry. He hadn't followed up on his letters, nor had he come to visit. Had his apology been a farce? If it was, could she still bring herself to forgive him?

Chapter Eleven

The familiar whistle sounded, and Katherine settled into her seat on the train. Six weeks had passed since the revival, and she was finally headed home on sabbatical. Pulling her Bible from her overnight case, she flipped to the book of John, her favorite.

What would her parents say to the news that she was now a Believer? The family had never been religious, attending church only on Easter and Christmas.

"Lord, give me the words to share your love with Mom, Dad, and Elizabeth." She closed her eyes. "And with Henry and his family, too." She may no longer be Henry's sweetheart, but he deserved to know the saving grace of Jesus.

"Talking to yourself, dearie?"

Katherine turned to the woman seated across the aisle. Her snow-white pompadour was tucked under a wide-brimmed, navy-blue hat tied under her chin with a light blue ribbon. A tiny bunch of bluebells nestled on one side of the rim.

"Sorry to disturb you, but I was praying. I'm a bit nervous about going home and sharing my new faith."

"A young-un in Christ, are you? For an old biddy like me, that's wonderful to hear. You're part of the next generation of saints."

Katherine giggled. "A saint? You wouldn't say that if you knew me."

The woman gestured to the vacant seat next to her, and Katherine moved to join her.

"We become saints when we join the family of God, dearie." She seemed to study Katherine for a moment. "Will your family be hostile to the gospel?"

"My parents have always supported me in whatever I do. I don't know about my sister, Elizabeth."

"I am Miss Carson. What is your name?"

"Katherine Newman. Miss Newman."

"Well, Miss Newman, it will be up to you to woo them into the kingdom. Sounds high and mighty, doesn't it? You just need to shine for Jesus, show them how He's changed you. They'll smell the sweet aroma of salvation and want His peace, too."

"It won't be that easy, will it?"

"No, it's rarely easy to get people to see their need for God. Especially if life is going fine." She pointed to Katherine's ringless finger. "Do you have a young man, dearie?"

Katherine's face warmed, and she shook her head.

"I'm judging from that blush of yours, there's a story to share."

"You don't want to hear my woes."

"This train ride is going to take a while." She patted Katherine's arm. "I've got all the time in the world."

Taking a deep breath, Katherine outlined her courtship and break up with Henry, Alice's arrival in Williams, and the current struggle to forgive Henry. "I know God forgave me, and He requires me to forgive others, but I can't seem to put down the hurt I've been carrying with me."

"Pride is a terrible thing, dearie. I know firsthand the damage a prideful soul can cause. But I also know if you don't forgive this young man, eventually you'll taste the bitter pill of regret."

Katherine crossed her arms. "How can you accuse me of being prideful? I'm the one who was wronged."

"Yes, you were wronged, but so was our Lord Jesus. He was wronged so badly, He ended up on a cross. But tell me this, why are you so upset about what happened? Is it because you loved Henry so much that you were devastated? Or is it because you were embarrassed? Embarrassed by what other people might think or say about the situation, them wondering if there was a good reason for your young man to walk away from you? That's pride talking."

Katherine shook her head. "You don't understand."

"But I do. You see, I had a young man once, just like you did. We were in love and talking about getting married. Then we had a deep misunderstanding, and I rejected him. Walked away from our love because of what I *thought* happened. By the time I discovered my perception was incorrect, I was filled with so much pride I refused to go to him. I didn't ask his forgiveness, and now it's too late."

"How can it be too late?"

"Because he's gone. He died in a mining accident. I can never make things right, but you can. Don't pass up the opportunity to heal your relationship. 'Blessed are the peacemakers.'"

Katherine stared out the window at the blur of scenery. Could she be a peacemaker? Of all the things God had asked of her, that would be the hardest.

Her father pulled the wagon to a stop in front of the house. Katherine threw aside the blanket and climbed to the ground. Shivering against the cold, she rotated her neck and rubbed her lower back. Between the constant jostling of the train and bucking of the conveyance, her body ached all over.

Screaming sounded from inside, and the door flew open. Elizabeth shot from the house like a cannon ball and enveloped Katherine. "You're home. I didn't think you'd ever get here. Are you positively exhausted?"

Katherine giggled and hugged her sister. "I'm worn out, but you have enough energy for both of us."

Mom stood in the doorway, a broad smile on her face. "You're looking well, daughter."

Extricating herself from Elizabeth's grip, Katherine hurried to her mother. "Not after two days on the train, but it's kind of you to say."

"I've coffee warming on the stove and fresh-baked cookies for the weary traveler."

Her father hefted Katherine's trunk onto his shoulder. "And none of us could have any until you arrived, so we're all quite pleased to see you."

Smiling, Katherine linked arms with Mom and Elizabeth and marched into the house. "Then we best get to it."

They entered living room, one of her favorite rooms in the house. Several colorful rugs were scattered on the floor. The couch was an old Queen Anne piece her mother had inherited from an aunt. It had been upholstered numerous times over the years and was currently covered in a rich green and gold floral print. The cherry-wood arms were worn smooth by the many hands that had rested on its cushions. Two mismatched, overstuffed chairs flanked the stone fireplace. Her mother's knitting sat in its usual basket, bright colored skeins of yarn nestled inside. Books were stacked on every surface. The mantel held mementos and pictures, and a large coffee table held her grandmother's pewter tea service and the newspapers her father perused every night. It was good to be home.

"Honey, are you all right?"

Katherine turned. Mom stared at her, concern etched on her face.

"I'm fine, Mom. How can the house be the same, yet feel so different?"

Her mother patted her arm.

Elizabeth entered the room. "Lunch is ready. Should I ring a gong, Katherine?"

"Very funny. I can manage to eat without the sound of a gong or a train. Although it might be too quiet here to sleep. What do you think?"

"Duly impressed. Now let's eat, I'm starving."

They seated themselves, and Katherine held out her hands. "I'd like to say grace, if you don't mind."

Her parents exchanged glances, and her father nodded.

Katherine bowed her head. "Dear God, thank You for bringing me home safely.

Thank You for my family. Please bless this food to our bodies. In Jesus name, amen." She looked at her parents. "I guess you thought that was odd of me to pray."

Dad wiped his mouth. "Your request took us off guard. We haven't been a praying family."

"I've only been praying for the last couple of months. I'd like to tell you about it."

Her parents nodded, but Elizabeth scowled and poked at her food.

Katherine wiped her damp hands on her skirt. Her breath caught, and she cleared her throat. "I attended a meeting at a church in Williams with my friend Eunice. The preacher talked about being hurt deep inside and how God could take that hurt away and help us with our burdens. I was tired of being angry about Henry's breakup with me. I was so weary from carrying all those bad feelings. So, I talked with the preacher and asked God to come into my life and change me. I'm a Believer now."

Her sister dropped her fork with a clatter. "So, you don't have any problems now? I find that hard to believe. Suddenly, everything is okay with Henry."

Katherine shook her head. "It's not like that at all. We're human beings. We're never going to get rid of our problems, but God helps us to deal with them. It's very hard to understand until you experience it."

Elizabeth crossed her arms. "Does this make you superior to us?"

"I'm sorry for not explaining this well. Maybe if you read my Bible."

"You read the Bible?" Her sister's voice was like ice.

Lord, help me. I'm messing this up. "Yes, I read the Bible. It helps me learn how to be a better person." She smiled. "I am still the same individual who left, but I'm different inside. What I've come to believe is that each person is created by God, but because of what Adam and Eve did we're all sinners. God sent His Son who is Jesus to earth as a sacrifice for us. When we ask Jesus to be in our heart, we become brand new. He is with me every moment of every day. When I feel hurt or tired or even overjoyed I share it with God." She pressed her lips together. Her parents looked non-committal, and Elizabeth wore a deep frown, her face dark and forbidding.

Just love them, child. It is not your job to save them.

Mom patted Katherine's arm. "We're glad you found God if that's what makes you happy, honey."

"I'm just—"

"Thank you for sharing, but let's talk about something else for a while." Dad peered at her over his glasses. "Your sister went to a lot of effort to prepare our meal."

"Yes, sir." Would her family ever see their need for God?

"I helped Mrs. Peabody deliver her grandchild." Mom's face glowed. "Dorothy had a beautiful baby girl. Of course, all babies are beautiful, aren't they?"

"Isn't that Dorothy's second?"

"Yes, she had a boy just after you left for Arizona. Those children are like day and night. He's a rough and tumble rambunctious boy. Amy is small and delicate. She hardly ever cries."

"Don't forget about Mr. O'Malley's nephew," Elizabeth said. "When his folks passed away, he came to live with him, but he gave them nothing but trouble. About a month ago, there was talk he was going to be sent away then he disappeared. No one has seen hide nor hair of him. We all figure we'll see his picture in the newspaper or in the post office someday."

"Elizabeth!"

"You know that's what people say, Mom."

"Well, maybe. But we should know better than to repeat it."

"It was the most excitement this town had seen in years. It's worth repeating. The only other decent news is Miss Reed, the librarian finally got married. She answered one of those mail order bride advertisements and found herself a man. She's living out in Oklahoma now on a big ranch."

"I've heard of that. We think some of the women we see coming through on the trains are mail order brides. Good for her. She's a nice woman." Katherine looked at her sister. "Why don't you answer one of those ads?"

Elizabeth lifted her chin. "Because I'm quite happy here without a husband. That could change, but I don't think I'm rancher's wife material. Do you?"

"There are more than just ranchers looking to get married, sis. You should check it out."

"Do you have everyone's life mapped out, Katherine?" Elizabeth pushed away her plate. "I'm done with this conversation. Please, excuse me." She stalked from the room.

Katherine's lower lip trembled. She hadn't been home long, and she had already offended her family. Had she been wrong to come home?

The following afternoon Katherine waved to her father who was repairing the fence that ran across the front of the property. Her family had attended church with her out of courtesy, but had failed to respond to the pastor's invitation. When she tried to discuss the sermon, Mom steered the conversation away from "this religion thing Katherine had found," and Elizabeth looked smug. Katherine was failing miserably at sharing the gospel with them.

Pulling her scarf closer to ward off the morning's chill, she trundled down the gravel road. The calendar might say it was Spring, but winter had not loosened its grip on Ohio yet. She kept to the side to avoid the ruts and bumps made by the wheeled traffic and lifted her face toward the cornflower-colored sky. The day held the promise of sunshine despite the frigid air. A hawk soared high above, and a rabbit darted through the fields oblivious to the winged danger.

Thirty minutes later she stood at the end of the lane that led to the Jorgensen's farm. Bowing her head, she prayed for guidance during the visit. She didn't want to bungle the conversation, as she had with her family.

She marched to the house and ascended the stairs to the front porch, her shoes clumping on the wood. Katherine tugged on the rope to ring the ship's bell a distant cousin had sent from one of his many trips abroad. A loud clang shattered the silence, and she winced.

The door opened. Olga Jorgenson swept Katherine into an embrace. "How wonderful to see you. When did you get home? Would you like to come in?"

"Thank you. I've come to speak with you and your family."

"Is everything all right?"

"Yes, I'll explain when we're together."

"Mr. Jorgensen and I are the only ones home at the moment. The children are in school, and Henry and Carl are away on business."

Katherine's step faltered. "Henry is away?"

"He works for the railroad, and his job takes him up and down the line. Why don't you sit down, and I'll get you some tea."

Katherine shook her head. "No, thank you. I won't take up much of your time."

"Very well, please join us in the parlor."

Mrs. Jorgensen led Katherine to a small room in the back of the house.

"Katherine wishes to speak with us."

Mr. Jorgensen put down his pipe, and his forehead wrinkled. "Katherine? We haven't seen you in over two years. What brings you here?"

She cleared her throat. Perhaps she should have accepted Mrs. Jorgensen's offer of tea. "First, I wanted to let you know that Alice sends her love. She misses you."

Olga leaned forward. "She was well when you left?"

"Yes, ma'am. She's making lots of friends, and she is a hard-working employee. It's been a joy to have her there." Tears filled her eyes. "I..ah…didn't always feel that way. I was angry at Henry for his breaking off our relationship, and I transferred those feelings to the rest of his family…to Alice…to you. I had very hateful feelings for your whole family. That was wrong of me, and I'm here to apologize for that." She ducked her head and sniffled.

Henry, Sr. waved his hand. "There is no need to apologize, Katherine. It is understandable you blamed your hurt on us as well."

"No, I must ask your forgiveness. I have sinned against you."

"Sinned?"

"Yes. I follow Jesus Christ now. Can I tell you about it?"

"Of course. And we forgive you, honey. We love you like our own daughters. We're sorry Henry hurt you. He let his pride get in the way of your relationship."

"I have my own struggles with pride." She shared her experience from the revival service and how God had cleaned up the mess she made of her life.

"You've given us a lot to think about, Katherine, but we're not ready to make any sort of commitment."

Clasping hands with Henry's parents, she smiled. "Thank you for listening." Rising, she picked up her shawl, and her gaze wandered to the mantel where a framed photograph of Henry and Katherine sat among the other pictures.

Studying their images, she waited for her anger to surface. Instead, a tinge of regret at what might have been brought tears to her eyes, then peace wrapped her in warmth. God had healed her. Would she get a chance to tell Henry?

At two o'clock, the train entered the station, whistle shrieking. Katherine's month-long sabbatical was over, and it was time to return to Arizona. Her mother clung to her arm while her father busied himself with loading her trunk into the baggage car. Elizabeth dug into her reticule and handed an envelope to Katherine. "For later."

Tucking the letter into her pocket, she embraced her family. "This visit has been such a blessing. I will miss you terribly."

"We love you honey. We'll be out to visit soon."

The whistle sounded again, and the porter called out, "Board!"

Katherine climbed onto the train and made her way to her seat. Pulling down the window, she reached out to wave. Minutes later, the engine gathered steam and chugged from the station. Her family faded from view, and she wiped tears from her face. She missed them already. Perhaps Elizabeth's letter would cheer her.

Dear Katherine:

By the time you read this, you will be on your way back to Arizona. I didn't want to say this in front of Mom and Dad, but I've decided to follow your Jesus.

Katherine clutched the paper to her chest. Hallelujah. Her sister was a Believer.

I wanted you to be the first to know. I will be praying for you, and I hope you'll be praying for me. I'm going to follow in your footsteps and become a teacher. I love little children and feel called to help them learn. I will be starting at the Teacher's Academy next month. Fortunately, Mom and Dad sent us both to college, so I only need a few classes to obtain my certificate.

You've made me realize I can do anything I put my mind to. I will tell Mom and Dad my news once you have departed. I didn't want to take any attention from you while you were home.

I love you, sis.

Sighing, Katherine sagged against the seat. It had been a wonderful visit. Her sister had found the Lord, and Jesus had healed Katherine of her anger. If only she had been able to see Henry, to tell him. Was he part of God's plan for her life? Just because she forgave him and still loved him, didn't mean they were to marry, did it? Or was he simply a lesson learned to carry through her life's journey?

Chapter Twelve

Katherine sifted through the paperwork that had collected during the month she had been gone. Despite sleeping soundly after her return yesterday, she yawned widely. It would take more than one night to recover from the strenuous journey. Perhaps a cup of coffee would wipe away her lethargy.

Entering the dining room, she gasped. Near the kitchen door, Mr. Byron Harvey, Fred's son, conversed with Miss Washington. *A surprise inspection!* Katherine smoothed her apron over her skirt and hurried to the man and held out her hand. "Mr. Harvey, it's an honor to have you with us."

"It's nice to see you again, Miss Newman. Always a pleasure to visit my facility in Williams. You and Miss Washington keep this place ship shape, just the way I like it."

Katherine's face warmed.

"I'm here to conduct a routine examination, but I'm sure everything will be perfect."

"We do our best, sir." Miss Washington said.

"Shall we get started?" He withdrew a pair of white cotton gloves from his pocket and pulled them onto his hands. Strolling among the tables, he studied their set-up. He spoke to patrons and periodically ran his finger across window sills, counters and railings.

Without a word, he walked to the lunch room and performed the same inspection.

Holding her breath as he seemed to study every inch of the building as well as the books, Katherine exchanged glances with Miss Washington. Would he find anything amiss?

Four hours later, Katherine and Miss Washington stood in the foyer awaiting the train that would spirit Mr. Harvey away.

He leaned on his walking stick and surveyed the opulent lobby. "As I suspected, I am well pleased with this House. There isn't a speck of dirt to be seen, the brass and pewter are gleaming, and the service is impeccable. Thank you, ladies, for your hard work and diligence adhering to my father's vision. You can expect a raise in your next paychecks."

Katherine's eyes widened. "A raise? Thank you for your generosity."

The train whistle wailed, and he pulled out his pocket watch. "Right on time." He tipped his hat and sauntered out the door.

Huffing out a deep breath, Katherine flopped onto an overstuffed burgundy sofa. "I'm glad that's over."

Miss Washington straightened her collar. "Me, too. I couldn't believe it when I sauntered into the dining room to find Mr. Harvey talking to one of the girls. I was sure he would say something about my tardiness."

"Maybe he thought you were conducting important Harvey Company business."

Giggling, Miss Washington pulled a lace-edged handkerchief from her pocket and dabbed her face. "Back to work for the two of us. I'll oversee the dining hall if you want to finish what you were doing in the office."

"Thank you. I've almost caught up. Another thirty minutes should do it."

"Take as long as you need. I'm sure the visit with your family is worth the extra work."

Katherine's breath caught, and she walked back to her office. Going home had been wonderful, but the stress of being back on the job and subjected to a surprise inspection made the trip seem like a distant memory already. What were her parents doing? Elizabeth?

"Lord, I love being Head Waitress. The challenge is exciting, and I'm learning so much. But is this where you want me? Was my visit home your way of telling me it's time to return to Warren so I can witness to my family?"

"Miss Newman, you're needed in the dining hall."

A month after returning from home, Katherine had settled back into her routine. She rose from the chair in her room and tucked the letter from Henry in her pocket. He had finally written, telling her about his job in the mines and his appreciation of her apology to his parents. Claiming he still loved her, he asked if he had any hope that she shared his feelings.

Did she?

Sighing, she followed the young woman downstairs and entered the dining hall.

Miss Washington stood next to Roy O'Leary, one of the new bus boys, their faces mirror images of anger.

"What seems to be the problem?"

Miss Washington gestured to Roy. "This morning, the assistant cook, one of the pantry boys, and two of the porters reported personal items missing from their rooms. I conducted a search and discovered the items under Mr. O'Leary's mattress.

"I didn't put them there. I'm being framed." He clenched his fists. "You don't like me because I'm Irish."

Katherine reared back as if slapped. "How can you say such a thing? There is no discrimination at the Harvey Company." She looked at Miss Washington. "We should contact Sheriff Bainbridge immediately."

Heavy footfalls sounded behind her. "It's already been done, missy. One of your maintenance boys fetched me." He walked to Roy and gestured for him to stand. "Come with me, son, and we'll see if we can sort this out."

Roy shoved his way past the sheriff and bolted out the door. His pounding steps faded.

Bainbridge crossed his arms and shook his head. "If he's not guilty, why's he running?"

"Shouldn't you go after him, Sheriff?"

A man hollered, and the sound of scuffling neared. Deputy Pine entered the room gripping Roy by one arm.

"I'd say the deputy has it all under control." The sheriff dipped his head. "We'll take it from here, ladies, but we will need to interview the staff who have been victimized."

Katherine's heart raced. "Certainly, Sheriff. We'll make them available." What else could go wrong?

A dark-haired porter hesitated at the doorway. He held up a telegram. "Miss Newman, this just came for you."

Katherine swayed and caught the back of the chair to keep from falling. Telegrams only meant one thing. Bad news. She nodded, and the man handed her the envelope. She stared at her name scrawled across the ivory paper in black ink.

Miss Washington waved her arm. "Please clear the room, gentlemen."

Seconds later the two were alone, and Miss Washington guided Katherine to the sofa. "Take a deep breath. We'll handle whatever is inside."

Licking her dry lips, Katherine bowed her head and prayed. *Dear Lord, is this another test of my faith? What difficulty must I face now?* She opened her eyes and slit the envelope with a fingernail. Slipping the paper from inside, she unfolded the message.

MOTHER ILL WITH PNEUMONIA. PROGNOSIS NOT GOOD. COME

HOME IMMEDIATELY.

Chapter Thirteen

As the train lumbered to a stop at the Reidsville station, Katherine searched the platform. Her father waited next to the wagon, his face lined and gray. She blinked back the tears that threatened to spill down her cheeks. Her mother's illness must be devastating to her father.

Grabbing her reticule and pocketbook, Katherine rushed from the car. She ran to her dad. "Mom? Is she—?"

"We are guardedly optimistic, honey. Her fever broke two days ago and hasn't returned. She's very weak, but the doctor thinks she'll recover. It will be a long road for her."

Katherine wilted. "I've been praying for her all the way home, dad."

Dad enveloped her in his arms, and they both cried. "We all have, honey. God has smiled on us and spared your mother."

She pulled back, gaping at her father.

"Yes, your mother and I have committed to your Jesus. I bargained a bit with him when she relapsed with her fever. I told God if he would spare your mother, I'd follow Him the rest of my life. When she came out of the fever, we both prayed for salvation."

"But did you mean it, Dad? You're a real believer?"

"I'm really a Believer, honey. I know now that it's a mighty powerful God who can heal us. More importantly, I realized He is a personal God when He healed your mother to give me the desires of my heart."

"You've made me the happiest girl in the world. Let's go see Mom."

They retrieved her trunk and hoisted it into the wagon before setting out for the house. The thirty-minute drive seemed to take nearly as long as the three-day train ride.

Katherine leaned forward willing the vehicle to move faster. As they rolled to a stop in front of the house, she vaulted out of the seat and jumped to the ground. She charged up the steps and through the front door.

Her mother was lying on the sofa propped against several large pillows. A multi-colored crazy quilt was wrapped around her slight body. Her face was pale, and she gave her daughter a wan smile. Katherine knelt on the floor and tentatively touched her other's hand. "I'm home now, Mom. I can help take care of you.

Katherine rose and went to her sister who sat in the far corner near the fire. "You must be exhausted. First, you had to finish school in a short time and now this. It's my turn to share the burden. Now that Mom is on the mend, you should pursue your dream."

"It's not been a burden. Mom took care of us through the years." She beamed. "But I have received two offers to teach, and I owe them an answer. They've been willing to wait, but I can't hold off my decision any longer."

Katherine sat on the hearth. "I want every detail."

Elizabeth laughed. "One of the schools is in a small community much like our own and groups the students together. There are about twenty-five students from grades one through six. The current teacher is leaving to get married. The other opportunity is a larger school. I would teach first and second grade only. They have about fifteen students. There are pros and cons for both positions."

"How exciting. Which way are you leaning?"

"It will be more challenging to run the one-room schoolhouse. The pay isn't nearly as good, but money isn't why I chose to teach."

"I enjoyed the spread in ages when I taught. It kept things from getting boring. You can also pace the children's learning as you need to, because you'll be in control of the situation."

"That's what I thought, too. I'll write the school administrators tonight to notify them of my selection." She flung off the quilt and stood up. "I feel like a whole new world has opened up to me."

Katherine nibbled her lower lip. Had her own world shrunk by returning home?

Dad came down the stairs. "I've put your trunk at the end of your bed, sweetheart. It's ready to unpack."

Elizabeth grabbed Katherine's hand, and the two bounded up the stairs. "I'll help you. We can catch up while we put away your things."

Emptying her trunk into the dresser against the wall, Katherine fingered one of the skirts she had purchased in Flagstaff. She closed the drawer and busied herself with the souvenirs she had brought home. As she put the small framed picture of Eunice and her on top of the desk, she studied the images.

"You miss your friends, don't you?"

"More than I thought I would." She shrugged. "At first, I was afraid to go to Arizona, and then I wanted to stay there. I wouldn't have come home if it weren't for Mom's illness. I fit in and was doing a job I loved. The other employees and I had become a team. We were one of the best Harvey Houses – Mr. Harvey said so himself."

"I'm sorry you had to come home."

"Don't be sorry."

"We were doing okay, until Mom's fever spiked. Henry is back in Warren with the railroad, and he's been coming over three days a week to help Dad."

Katherine stilled, but her heart raced. "Henry comes to the house? Why would he do that?" Did Elizabeth hear the strain in her voice?

"He's changed. Working for the railroad has matured him. Maybe the pain of losing you, too. I don't know, but whatever happened, he seems to be a new man. Dad says he's a big help. Didn't he tell you?"

"No."

"Maybe he was waiting for the right time."

Would there ever be a right time to see Henry?

Katherine pulled the rope that lowered the attic stairs and climbed into the garret. It was mid-morning, so the temperature in the small enclosure was still bearable. Three weeks has passed since her return home, and Mom was on the mend. Able to sit up for longer periods of time each day, she could walk to a chair on the porch. "Where are those boxes I packed before moving to Arizona?"

A desk that had seen better days was shoved in one corner. Made of pine, it was stained with a dark pecan finish. There were three drawers on the right and an oblong one to the left. "I don't remember that piece of furniture. Wonder who it belonged to?"

She opened the first drawer and jumped back as a mouse scurried over the edge. Wiping her hands on her skirt, she banged on the second drawer and listened for any noise. Hearing nothing, she grinned and opened it.

Empty.

The third drawer held photos of her mother and another young woman standing in front of a building. Sliding them in her pocket, she opened a crumbling ledger book. She flipped through pages filled with tiny, cramped handwriting. The columns listed produce and livestock and associated pricing. Must have been Grandpop's.

Continuing to explore the loft, she worked from one side to the other. Many of the boxes contained clothing she and her sister had outgrown over the years. With her mother's love of quilting, the contents would eventually be converted to beautiful works of art.

The temperature rose, and Katherine mopped the perspiration from her face. She glanced at her watch. Two hours had passed. Pulling one of the remaining cartons toward herself, she opened it and found an ivory satin gown. "This doesn't belong to Mom. Who would leave a wedding dress in our attic?"

Shaking her head, she went to the final box by the window. Pressing her lips together, she wrapped her arms around her middle. Her box of mementos. Did she want to walk down Memory Lane?

She took a deep breath and removed the lid. Tears filled her eyes, and her vision blurred. The paper fan Henry had won for her at the carnival lay on top. Holding the faded souvenir to her chest, Katherine sobbed. She was lying to herself insisting she no longer loved Henry. His letter claimed he still cared for her, but that had come months ago.

Did she still have a chance?

Katherine scrubbed the house from top to bottom. The windows were open wide, and the curtains fluttered merrily in the breeze. She walked onto the porch to join her mother who shelled peas into a ceramic bowl.

Leaning the broom against the doorframe, Katherine stretched. "Folks should be here in a couple of hours for Elizabeth's party."

"You've done a magnificent job preparing. It will be an event people remember for a while. I know it means a lot to Elizabeth you are doing this for her."

"I'm going to miss her. Now I'll know how you all felt while I was in Arizona.

It's always harder being left behind, isn't it?"

"It can be."

Katherine squinted into the sunshine and picked up an oval-shaped basket. Checking her apron pocket to ensure her shears were inside, she headed down the steps. "I'm going to clip some flowers for the dining room table." She wandered from garden to garden choosing her sister's favorites. Lily of the Valley, marigold, daisies, goldenrod and black-eyed Susans went into the basket. Some of her mother's roses were still blooming, and Katherine bent low to smell the velvety fragrance.

"Katherine?"

Jumping at the sound, Katherine looked up.

Henry stood in the grass, his hat gripped in his hands. His crystal blue eyes were riveted on her face.

She drank in the planes of his face and the curl of his hair. Swallowing, she shook her head. Glancing toward the porch, she frowned at her mother's vacant chair. "Henry, what are you doing here?"

"I came to see you. We've been avoiding each other for too long."

She took a deep breath. "How have you been?" Could he hear her heart pounding in her ears?

"I'm fine, Katherine. It's wonderful to see you." His warm, baritone voice was like a melody.

Her palms began to sweat, and she chided herself. "Would you...ah...like to sit down?"

"I'd rather go for a walk if you're not too tired. I thought our reunion should be a little less public."

"All right. Let me put these flowers in the house and tell my parents where I'll be." Her steps paused. "Where will I be?"

He chuckled, and the dimples in his cheeks deepened. "How about if we walk down to the pond at the edge of your folk's property?"

"Ok, I'll be right back." Did she sound calmer than she felt?

Moments later she emerged from the house, and the pair ambled toward the water.

Henry led her to the small wooden bench her father had built five years ago. Katherine sat down and removed her hat. Fanning herself with it, she looked at Henry. Her insides quivered like a spring ready to snap.

Henry fiddled with the coins in his pockets; a sure sign of his own anxiety. He paced for a moment and then stopped abruptly. He went down on one knee and took her hands in his.

"Katherine, we have a lot to discuss. I hope since you were willing to see me that you want to iron things out."

She nodded unable to trust her voice.

Tucking a stray hair behind her ear, he stroked her cheek. "First and foremost, I need to ask your forgiveness for the way I treated you. I was filled with pride and unable to accept help from anyone. We were sinking financially, and in my mind, I needed to be able to support my family before I could ask you to share my life. I have since learned how foolish I was. A husband and wife are partners, and I should have been able to share my feelings and concerns with you so we could have worked them out together. Can you find it in your heart to forgive me, Katherine?"

Tears trickled down her cheeks. "I forgive you, Henry."

He wiped away the wetness from her face. "There's more I need to say before I can ask you to be my wife. I would not have wished the last three years on us, but I am a better man for them. I have learned to follow Jesus as Lord in my life and I—""

Katherine lunged forward to hug him, and they tumbled to the ground.

"What is it?"

She alternated between laughing and crying. "Henry, I'm a Believer, too!"

"Your parents told me after they accepted him, too." He helped her to her feet before propping himself on one knee. "Katherine Newman, would you do me the honor of consenting to be my wife?"

Chapter Fourteen

"I would love to marry you, Henry Jorgensen."

Henry leapt to his feet and embraced Katherine. "There's much to share."

Katherine put her fingers to Henry's lips. "And I can't wait, but today must be about Elizabeth. Let's wait to make our announcement until tomorrow. Will that be okay?"

The creak of wagons and carts carried from the driveway.

He grinned. "It will have to be. The festivities have begun."

The pair walked back to the house arm in arm. Her father and mother greeted the visitors, and Elizabeth sat under the large oak tree in the front yard surrounded by her friends.

When the last guest had arrived, George called for them to form a circle. Young and old clasped hands as they came together. He bowed his head and prayed, "Dear God, thank You for all who have come here to celebrate Elizabeth's new life. Thank You for keeping our friends safe during their travels. Thank You for the food which we are about to eat. Most of all we thank You for Your Son who You sent to die for us. In Jesus name we pray, Amen."

The crowd dispersed and lined up at the buffet tables. The noise became a murmur as people filled their plates and began eating. After the children had their fill, they raced around the yard. The afternoon wore on, people visited with each other and caught up on the latest news. Elizabeth was the center of attention as people quizzed her about where she was going and what she would be doing.

Near the end of the afternoon, Dad announced it was time to hit the piñata. Children gathered from all over the yard to take turns swinging the hickory stick at the candy-filled form. The crowd cheered as one-by-one the youngsters were blindfolded and given the pole to take a chance. Several of the smaller children managed to make contact with the piñata, and it was beginning to show signs of wear.

Finally, Billy Thornton stepped up to take his turn. At thirteen he was tall for his age and had already proven his abilities with a bat and ball.

Mr. Newman tied the black cotton blindfold around his eyes.

"Can you see anything, Billy?"

"No, sir!"

"Ok." Rotating the young man several times, Mr. Newman pushed him toward the papier-mâché toy.

CRACK!

Billy hit the piñata, and it split in half. The adults applauded, and the children surged forward to collect the fallen candy. Billy ripped off his blindfold and joined the chaos. The children giggled and wrestled with each other in an effort to collect the most candy. Billy held aloft a small wrapped box.

"Hey, Miss Newman. There's a present in here for you!" He waved the gift in the air.

"What? How do you know it's for me?"

He rolled his eyes. "It's got your name on it."

She rushed over and plucked it from his hands. "Where in the world did this come from? I filled the piñata myself."

Tearing off the wrapping paper, she found a small blue velvet box. She opened it, and a solitaire diamond ring set in a white gold band glittered in the sun. Finding Henry in the crowd, she smiled in response to the self-satisfied grin he wore.

"I thought we weren't going to announce anything."

"You thought wrong." he laughed. "I purchased the ring in the hopes you would agree to marry me. I brought it over this morning to give to you after everyone left.

Elizabeth got wind of things and insisted we put it in the piñata. She wanted to be part of the announcement before she left."

"This is such a surprise."

"I hope to keep surprising you the rest of our lives."

She waggled her eyebrows at him. "Only good surprises."

He dropped a resounding kiss on her lips, and the crowd roared with laughter.

The End

What did you think of *On the Rails?*

Thank you so much for purchasing *On the Rails?* You could have selected any number of books to read, but you chose this book.

I hope it added encouragement and exhortation to your life. If so, it would be nice if you could share this book with your family and friends by posting to one or more of your favorite social media outlets.

If you enjoyed this book and found some benefit in reading it, I'd appreciate it if you could take some time to post a review on Amazon, Goodreads, BookBub or other book review site of your choice. Your feedback and support will help me to improve my writing craft for future projects and make this book even better.

Thank you again for your purchase.

Blessings,

Linda Shenton Matchett

Acknowledgments

Although writing a book is a solitary task, it is not a solitary journey. There have been many who have helped and encouraged me along the way.

My parents, Richard and Jean Shenton, who presented me with my first writing tablet and encouraged me to capture my imagination with words. Thanks, Mom and Dad!

Scribes212 – my ACFW online critique group that got me started on this journey: Valerie Goree, Marcia Lahti, and the late Loretta Boyett (passed on to Glory, but never forgotten). Without your input, my writing would not be nearly as effective.

Eva Marie Everson – my mentor/instructor with Christian Writers' Guild. You took a timid, untrained student and turned her into a writer. Many thanks!

SincNE, and the folks who coordinate the Crimebake Writing Conference. I have attended many writing conferences, but without a doubt, Crimebake is one of the best. The workshops, seminars, panels, critiques, and every tiny aspect are well-executed, professional, and educational.

Special thanks to Hank Phillippi Ryan, Halle Ephron, and Roberta Isleib for your encouragement and spot-on critiques of my work.

Paula Proofreader (https://paulaproofreader.wixsite.com/home): I'm so glad I found you! My work is cleaner because of your eagle eye. Any mistakes are completely mine.

Thanks to my Book Brigade who provide information, encouragement, and support.

A heartfelt thank you to my brothers, Jack Shenton and Douglas Shenton, and my sister, Susan Shenton Greger for being enthusiastic cheerleaders during my writing journey. Your support means more than you'll know.

My husband, Wes, deserves special kudos for understanding my need to write. Thank you for creating my writing room – it's perfect, and I'm thankful for it every day. Thank you for your willingness to accept a house that's a bit cluttered, laundry that's not always done, and meals on the go. I love you.

And finally, to God be the glory. I thank Him for giving me the gift of writing and the inspiration to tell stories that shine the light on His goodness and mercy.

Other Titles by this Author

Romance

Love's Harvest, Wartime Brides, Book 1
Love's Rescue, Wartime Brides, Book 2
Love's Belief, Wartime Brides, Book 3
Love's Allegiance, Wartime Brides, Book 4

Spies & Sweethearts, Sisters in Service, Book 1
The Mechanic & The MD, Sisters in Service, Book 2
The Widow & The War Correspondent, Sisters in Service, Book 3

Gold Rush Bride Hannah, Gold Rush Brides, Book 1
Gold Rush Bride Caroline, Gold Rush Brides, Book 2
Gold Rush Bride Tegan, Gold Rush Brides, Book 2

Dinah's Dilemma, Westward Home & Hearts Mail Order Brides
Rayne's Redemption, Westward Home & Hearts Mail Order Brides
Daria's Duke, Westward Home & Hearts Mail Order Brides
Ellie's Escape, Westward Home & Hearts Mail Order Brides

Vanessa's Replacement Valentine, Brides of Pelican Rapids
A Family for Hazel, Brides of Pelican Rapids

Legacy of Love, Keepers of the Light

A Bride for Seamus, Proxy Bride Series
A Bride for Keegan, Proxy Bride Series

Estelle's Endeavor, Thanksgiving Books & Blessings Series, Collection 5

Maeve's Pledge, The Suffrage Spinsters Series

Dial V for Valentine, You're On the Air Series

Dial S for Second Chances, You're On the Air Series

Love at First Flight
Love Found in Sherwood Forest
On the Rails: A Harvey Girls Story
A Love Not Forgotten
A Doctor in the House

Mystery
Under Fire, Ruth Brown Mystery Series, Book 1
Under Cover, Ruth Brown Mystery Series, Book 2
Under Ground, Ruth Brown Mystery Series, Book 3

Murder of Convenience, Women of Courage, Book 1
Murder at Madison Square Garden, Women of Courage, Book 2

Non-Fiction
WWII Word Find, Volume 1

Let's Connect!

www.LindaShentonMatchett.com

www.facebook.com/LindaShentonMatchettAuthor

www.pinterest.com/lindasmatchett

www.linkedin.com/in/authorlindamatchett

https://www.amazon.com/Linda-Shenton-Matchett/e/B01DNB54S0

https://www.goodreads.com/author_linda_matchett

https://www.bookbub.com/authors/linda-shenton-matchett

Interested in more historical fiction?
Visit http://www.lindashentonmatchett.com/p/books.html

www.ingramcontent.com/pod-product-compliance
Lightning Source LLC
Chambersburg PA
CBHW021550150726
47990CB00006B/2473